ANTEROS

Daniel Vogel

ANTEROS

DOUBLE DRAGON

Chapter 1: Understory

Once a month, Ben's sleeping thoughts would defy a very sharp, subconscious command and plunge him into the nightmare. He'd never been able to remember that much of it, certainly not to the detail of subjects or behaviors or storylines. There were people in it, appearing only as gray shadows against the black backdrop. He was watching a theatrical play with all of the stage lighting turned off. These wispy, ghost-like beings danced around in near silence. They were singing to him, but he could never hear their message. Whatever they were trying to convey was important, this he knew. The only words he ever recalled were his own just as the terror was about to suddenly start. He screamed in such an agonized and distorted way that he didn't even know it was himself at first.

"OH MY GOD, I'M CUT IN HALF!"

Ben Porterfield threw himself back into the world. Lying on his back, he was immediately pounded by that hot, deep humidity from all sides. A thick film of salty sweat was sandwiched between his back and the bed sheets. Every morning he awoke soaking, since the air conditioner was mostly rebuilt, but not enough to actually get the damn thing running. His own shriek in the dream still echoed in his ears with such intensity that he could hear it as clearly as if it had been spoken right next to him. But this time it wasn't just the monthly night terror that bothered him, it was that they were getting worse -more horror, more extreme personal pain. His current job certainly had the possibility of injury, which could be the reason for the faster tempo. And then there was that awful disappearance, Bill Paginot, who'd turned up missing two days ago on the trail that passed right in front Ben's house. To add to the anxiety of it all, he was practically the only safety officer on the planet.

In the mirror he looked at the middle-aged man and felt even older than that at times. He'd spent eighteen months in some kind of frozen sleep, and for the rest of that time he was wandering around that cruiser looking for something to do. Ben needed to lose twenty-five, maybe thirty pounds, the weight gained on the trip, and it was really starting to present itself, since there just wasn't much to keep an insomniac active when cooped up on a transport. He was only forty-three, and a quarter of his light brown hair had already turned grey -not a good sign. There were always meds, one pill would take care of the hair for an entire year, but what the hell was the point? He looked at the expressionless reflection staring back at him and realized again that every day he recognized himself less and less. The most important part of his life was that he was married to someone who did, and always would.

Police uniforms differed from state to state, colony to colony, depending on the terrain. In North Dakota, it was a standard Army-looking dessert kaki pattern. Here, it was dark blue, with a similar jacket and cap. The NAS State Department's Settlement safety office must have been smoking something when mandating a jacket here, he thought, because in this kind of heat, it was impossible to wear. This morning, Ben wore it for all of ten seconds before tossing it into a pile of clothes in the closet and rolling up the sleeves of the light blue shirt. In the absence of a jacket, he clipped the circular badge onto his belt. It was the best he could do, and the nearest auditor was quite some distance away.

Also on his belt was a holster with two guns. He had the Chambers 4.25 millimeter, something he'd never used on anyone in his twenty years of law enforcement. From its fifty-round magazine, it electromagnetically propelled a medium-high fragmenting bullet made from a carbon-laced-steel core to a velocity of around four thousand feet per second. It was an 8-inch-barrelled, hand-held railgun that theoretically was accurate up to twelve hundred yards, not like that meant anything in a rainforest. And then in the holster aft of the pistol he had the shorter six-inch stun gun. Pretty effective –it created a narrow-beam neuro-electric pulse that could bring a moose down for a minute or so, but that was all it had been designed to do.

He stepped out onto the front porch, surprised by the kaleidoscopic walls of blue and green flora that exploded into his field of vision. Trees and flowers were everywhere, yet none of them familiar. *AN ALIEN PLANET!* He longed for the dry and cool town of Grand Forks. He had grown up reading books and newspaper articles about living on other worlds, an endeavor not all that spectacular anymore. For many decades people had journeyed from Earth to its twenty nearest star systems, with hundreds of different mining or green house colonies to choose from. But these planets were barren of air and life. Most of Earth's interstellar colonial networks possessed hot planets like Mercury, or places wrapped in blankets of CO_2 like Venus, or gaseous monsters like Jupiter and Saturn. Before the discovery of this world, there had been nothing similar to the Earth, with a breathable atmosphere. People had gotten used to the idea of thick and bulky pressure suits, encasing men and women as they clumsily bobbed up and down on some gray, cratered surface, devoid of oxygen and water, from one life support bubble to the next. But not here, since this planet had air.

A hundred and ten years ago the Gorgon Nebula had been discovered, a vast region of space thick with gas and dark matter. Hidden behind it was a magnificent binary white-red star system, hosting twelve planets in orbit. It had taken the unmanned U.S. Astro Space explorer *Bolthor* twenty years to get here, and it discovered that the fourth planet in orbit was covered with a lush bluish-green verdure. *Bolthor*, with its primitive, century-old fusion-matter expulsion drive, had returned to Earth over forty years after it had departed, carrying its treasure trove of computer information on a planet later to be christened Anteros.

And then the First Survey came, followed by the Second, the people who had first set foot here. These trailblazers had been the builders and geologists, and with their pre-fab kits had put up hundreds of structures and houses that now comprised their home. But more than half of the first people who'd colonized Anteros had disappeared, a horrific fact that had been only revealed to Ben two months earlier when he landed with the Third Survey. The people had been consumed by the rainforest, but not even the remaining survivors knew what had become of them. When Ben and the rest of his group of colonists arrived, they found a nearly-empty, decaying town, left to the whims and mercy of the jungle. The man who was supposed to have been his boss had been presumed killed long ago. Although it hadn't been stated in his original job description, Ben was now the chief safety officer, and it was his job to figure out what happened to these people, and how to prevent it from happening to the Third Survey. But now another person was lost, someone he'd known.

Ben looked at the trees, vines and flowers. The panorama of his front yard made the memory of North Dakota seem like that of a desert. His former home had been wheat-brown and quiet. Its early morning sounds consisted of the distant electric hum of cars whizzing along inside a glass-enclosed highway, two-hundred floors below where Ben had stood on his open balcony. Voices from down there could not be heard. There were interstate birails – long cylinders that stretched to infinity in both directions -channels for silent trains going thousands of miles an hour. Stratohoppers, the disc-shaped, wingless hovercraft, could have shattered the very foundation of his apartment building with their thunderous noise, but they engaged their magnetic generators at such an altitude that they, too, were almost without noise.

On the planet Anteros, the voices were numerous and very loud. There was the chattering of crickets and beetles, the warbling of enormous, unseen birds, and the suspicious rustling of tropical brush by the unknown animals that roamed the surface of this very odd world. The wood making up the two-by-fours on the porch floor was white with a bluish tint, a strong timber that had been used in the construction of the entire house. Ben walked down the steps, listening with dissatisfaction as they squeaked and moaned beneath his weight. The front yard was a small one, leading out thirty feet before intersecting a muddy bike trail carved out of the brush. Trees reached up like so many titan fingers pointing up at the sky, most higher than nine hundred feet. Pinnacles, as they were called, were the tallest trees any human being had ever laid eyes on. They formed a tight mesh of branches at the top, effectively absorbing most of the sunlight with their circular, massive leaves.

When Ben reached the trail he turned around to gaze at his house from a distance. He was too much of a perfectionist and had a bad habit of nitpicking, having slaved behind manual hammers and hand saws for two months in what little spare time he had since the interstellar lander had dropped down from orbit and deposited him there. He had rebuilt a good part of this dwelling, using blue wood panels and gray wood for molding. He looked down the dark and gloomy trail, which would accommodate hovering transports, light bikes and pedestrians, but nothing larger. Then he heard creaking on the porch and light thumps on the stairs. Janice Porterfield had been working in the back yard and saw that he was up.

Her bright red hair was a lovely contrast to the surroundings, advertising "I'm here!" Thirty-six years old, Ben thought, and hasn't changed at all since college. The only time Ben ever used the words "love" and 'beautiful' was when he thought of his wife. Her kindness coupled with sarcasm made her so. She was wearing another very neutral gray jump suit. She'd always loved the yellow one, but discovered that the Anteros-equivalent of moths were also partial to this color, and changed her habits begrudgingly. These new outfits still revealed her slender physique. She had a prominent smile that was, it seemed, a contrast to the world at times. Her hair flowed like a river half-way down her back, but she refused to compromise on this, even if the red also attracted insects. She just sprayed more. Some things just can't be changed. Her feet sank into the moist soil as she made her way over to him, her sincerity the only friendly thing in this environment.

"Good morning," she said, wrapping her arms around his waist. He was large, a foot taller than her, and was now over twice her weight.

"Morning, Jan," he answered. "I had that dream, the nasty one."

Her smile diminished. "I guess it's over for a while longer. You'll be able to sleep better knowing that. Still like before?"

"The subject, if you can call it that, is the same. But it's getting more severe, I guess. I woke up with a pretty sharp pain in my stomach. That's never happened before."

"That was from me to you for hogging the bed," Jan smirked. Ben smiled.

"You're so nice, gentle, too." She looked a bit more serious.

"A missing person case doesn't help. A lot of missing persons, really, but this one just happened. How long has it been since you had to work something like this?"

"Oh, years. Years and years, but I always had to keep looking until I understood what had happened. That will be how it is now. I'll find out what's going on."

"I know you will, my love."

They both looked at the house, originally built by the construction crew who had since vanished or left when that massive, wonderfully-air-conditioned stellar hotel that had once been above returned home. Ben and Janice received permission to move into this dwelling, which was half-collapsed at the time and had tropical vines and branches poking into every window. It took many weeks of off-hours work, but it was starting to be habitable again. The front porch stretched across the entire facade, but the one-by-ones supporting the bannister were unevenly spaced enough so that it was very noticeable. They both looked up at the porch roof. It was crooked, standing eight feet above the porch on the right side, and eight and a half on the left. If they were looking at it from five hundred feet away, it would still look askew. Janice started to laugh.

"Dammit," Ben solemnly said. This made her really laugh. "This is just dumb. Nobody puts on a roof that bad."

"I know a couple of people who did," Jan broke in, "working in the dark and getting romantic. Guess that took our minds off carpentry."

"To hell with it. I think it looks fantastic."

"So do I."

"Let's go to town."

"Let's." Ben started walking toward the small garage, but Janice stepped onto the path. "I want to walk, Treefall is only ten minutes away."

"Thirty seconds by light bike." But Janice turned and brought her arms around him in a hug.

"Ben, I really want to get to know this place, and seeing the trees and animals zipping by in a speed blur doesn't do anything for me. We were in hibernation or otherwise stuck on that ship for two years to get here, and you've been working constantly since we landed. You gave yourself three whole hours off this morning before going back, so let's just take a real stroll. Anyhow, you need the exercise, you're getting a little tubby." Ben felt his smile stretching his face.

"Please, don't sugar-coat it like you usually do, let me know how you really feel." They both laughed. Janice was the most honest person he'd ever known, but they had settled on a planet that swallowed up new-comers. *HOW AM I SUPPOSED TO RELAX?* Ben had just left a very difficult life behind him. He made a mistake once

13

twenty years ago, and the ghost of it followed him wherever he went, even to Anteros.

They had always planned on having the two-child maximum on Earth, and Ben could think of no potential parent better than she would be, with her profoundly thoughtful and brilliant nature, just someone who had "people-smarts." In all the time he'd known her, she had never even raised her voice, nor did he. For twelve years they had planned it out back home, and for those years their apartment remained devoid of the small feet of children running around with their high-pitched screams of joy and pain and growth. Now, Benjamin Porterfield was retired, his old life trillions of miles away. It was time to finally enter the most important phase of their marriage and lives, this was very true.

They started walking down the trail.

"I told Dean Ervin we'd pick him up at the clinic for brunch," Jan said, knowing that would bring out a politely negative response from Ben. He slouched a little.

"That's good."

"You don't really care for him, I sense that every time I even mention his name. He really is a very, very nice person, Ben. You just need to get to know him."

"I like the guy and think he's okay, I'm just tired of getting an earful of his life's story every time I get within a hundred yards of him. He wants to be everyone's friend, always too eager to please, and just seems kind of pretentious. I'm just not sure about him." Janice did not like hearing this. She had

14

stopped by Doctor Ervin's office several times, occasionally with her allergies, but in her last visit, which was definitely a more a severe case of anemia, she had been almost instantly cured. The good-natured Dean, with a joke and a dermal pad, removed the problem and the fear. She had developed an extremely good friendship with him.

"You'll need him around some day. You'll break a bone in your foot or get some parasite inside of you or get bitten, and then you'll need him professionally. He can be counted on, Ben, to help out in a bad time." He looked at her, and she continued. "And not just a bad time in a medical sense. Trust me, you two are going to be really good friends before long."

"Could happen."

"People change." He felt a twinge of denial that. *I HAVEN'T, IN TWENTY YEARS!* He had hoped that some of his memories of Earth, like a radio signal passing through the soupy Gorgon Nebula, would become distorted and unreadable. Many messages were painful, but Ben now realized that they were being transmitted as clearly as though coming from a broadcasting tower sitting right next to his sloppily assembled cabin.

They walked. It hadn't rained much and the trees were shedding unnecessary weight, dropping their thick, heavy leaves. Most of them were dark blue on top and pearly white underneath, with thick veins throughout. If one of those leaves landed right, Ben thought, it would wrap completely around my head. They plummeted to earth quickly, and after falling for hundreds of feet, made quite a racket when they struck the ground. Janice looked up while she walked and smiled.

"I can't see the moon." Ben looked up. The tropical rain forests, like any found on Earth, were dark, and here the branches were so high up Ben couldn't see them individually. Sunlight poked through holes and crevices so that the upper canopy was more like a pin cushion with brilliant light streaming through a few openings. "Every time I'm in town and see that moon, it rattles me a little, even though I've seen it now a few hundred times," she continued. The moon, Pallor, was red and heavily cratered, and three times the size of Earth's moon. Its orbit also held it very close to Anteros.

"We'll see it in Treefall," Ben answered. A lunar eclipse on Earth was a rare event, to be studied with a vengeance every few years. Anteros had one almost every week, lasting for several hours.

To the left and right of them were trees. It was more than a mere forest, since the trunk diameters of pinnacles were over a hundred feet. They walked alongside one, barely able to make out its curvature. It was more like strolling past a great wooden wall, with thick layers of moss covering its smooth bark. Ben felt small and insignificant next to this wooden mammoth. This tree had been standing there since before the Druids had constructed Bluestone Circle on Earth; it had been pummeling the surface with colossal leaves before the birth of Christ. For thousands of years this very tree had formed an immense home, motel and sanctuary for countless species of animals and insects. No one knew just how old these titans could get, but there were several growing near the settlement that dated back to the Earth's Stone Age.

In between there was darkness, the sunlight obscured by their shadows. There were maybe twenty yards of clear visibility, but beyond this were animal noises, none of them familiar. Ben felt a queasy dread just looking into this blackness - something could spring at him before he could react. Maybe that was how the other colonists had met their end. But Janice knew the tropics, having spent years in the Amazonian Tropical Rain Forest Reserve, not to mention the parks in Costa Rica and Ecuador. Diving into dense, unknown brush was her forte. In fact, it had been her job at the Smithsonian Tropical Research Institute that brought her and Ben to Anteros. Staring into the void between two trees, she sniffed at something, and then deeply inhaled. She suddenly jumped off the trail.

"Follow me," she said.

"Jan," She was gone, treating this dangerous environment as she would an expedition in Peru. He felt a sharp pain in his stomach. *AND ONE DAY SHE MIGHT NEVER RETURN.*

"Over here! It's a clearing!" Ben pushed his way through the cobweb-like moss and fumbled over roots of trees, which he had to climb rather than step over. Everything was so dark, and the thick vines and leaves tangled his feet. Then suddenly -sunshine! The two suns burned through the sky. Smaller trees and shrubs riddled a vast plain, but here there were no immense pinnacles cloaking the stars. This field stretched on for a

17

couple of miles before the trees again ruled. Janice stood fifty yards away. "Right here," she said. Ben walked over and gazed at the flowers hugging the ground that were arranged in a big circle, almost as if in a defensive congregation. In contrast to the dismal surroundings, their four-foot long ovoid petals exploded in brilliant orange and were nearly-glowing along the edges. To say they had a thin coat of cilia wasn't enough: these flowers had fur.

"Wow," Ben exclaimed. Its smell dominated the air, a fire-hose of scent, its intense fragrance overwhelming his nostrils and lapping at his tongue. Jan was next to it, savoring it.

"This is called a Freyja plant, and it's almost mythical, pouring out nectar. They only grow in open stretches of light and never in the shade, but there is nothing else like them." Ben approached, appreciating the enormity of this plant as Janice knelt next to it. She could lie down flat, and her length would still be shorter than the diameter of this thing. Ben felt like a field mouse observing an earth rose. He walked over to a second Freyja flower. These things were magnificent -that was obvious- and he wanted one for the living room.

"There is a woman in this field whose fiery beauty surpasses all of these flowers tenfold," Ben said, reaching over. Janice didn't look.

"You're such a flirt." She was instinctively trying to count the number of plants dotting the field when she heard her husband say, "Uh-oh."

"What?"

"I've got a problem." She turned and saw him stooped over a plant with his thumb planted in the

18

middle where the petals joined, and was struggling. "Jan, I'm stuck. This flower just grabbed me." She walked over to him and observed a gummy substance wrapped around his thumb and holding it fast.

"I'll guess that the gooey stuff is part of what's called mucilage. It's sticky."

"Damn right it's sticky." Ben pulled. The top of the flower, petals and all, rose with his hand, but the roots still held fast. "This thing's got my thumb and wants to keep it."

"The mucilage holds onto insects that land on it, until they can be gradually pulled down into the Freyja's stalk and digested. I'm sorry, didn't I mention that these plants are carnivorous?"

"Must have slipped your mind," Ben answered with a slight smile.

"These are called fly paper traps, and, my darling, I guess today, you're its fly!" she giggled. Ben really tugged this time, using his two-hundred-plus-pounds to jerk this flower as hard as he could. They could hear the plant stretching out, sounding like a rope being tugged on by a very heavy weight. It raised another few inches, but didn't relinquish its hold. Ben released his pull and Janice exploded in laughter.

"I think you two make a lovely couple," she said. "Inseparable." She laughed more. Ben did to and said,

"To have and to be held, 'till death do us part." He reached into his back pocket and pulled out a small pocketknife.

They moved back into the woods. A thousand-foot tree had hundreds of thousands of wooden arms tenaciously grabbing its neighbors. Whenever several of these trees died and fell, they would take a few extra comrades to the grave with them. The result was a large sunny opening called a treefall. One of these areas served as a settlement for all of the colonists from Earth, and was appropriately named Treefall. Bright purplish-white sunlight shined down on the town, looking much like an area on a wall that was illuminated by a flashlight in an otherwise unlit room. With the rays came a fulmination of living things. Treefall had struck Ben as looking like an ancient boom town of the American West or Russian Siberia. There were mud-soaked streets meandering between wooden buildings of questionable support. There was also a sense of fear inspired by the billions of animals that lurked beyond the safety of town limits, worsened with the knowledge that something out there had taken so many earlier colonists. The ghost-town state of Treefall they'd taken up residence in eight weeks ago had been an unexpected surprise waiting for these surveyors who had come from a world where every square centimeter had been mapped and recorded, where every animal larger than a ground hog had to be sheltered in special reserves to prevent its extinction. *NOW, WE ARE THE ANIMALS WHO NEED A PROTECTIVE ENCLAVE*. The five-hundred and seventeen men and women who had accompanied him, in addition to the forty-six people from the Second Survey who had stayed, would all-to-soon discover what true fear was. There were unknown entities waiting to meet them out there. *HOW WILL THEY, OR I, REACT IN A TRULY LIFE-THREATENING SITUATION?* He'd had known such an incident once back on Earth, and liked himself a lot less when remembering how he dealt it.

The Third Survey had brought many vehicles, mostly light bikes, but also three dozen narrowly-built human and cargo transports for the trails, like the two ambulances parked in front of the Treefall Hospital, the largest structure in town. It was three stories high and constructed from very precisely-cut two-by-fours of bluewood. Unimaginative rows of windows lined each floor, tinted black for privacy, but the inside it reeked of cleanliness. Ben's life now had been submerged in vanished people, but none of those folks had turned up at the clinic, so it was very quiet. Occasionally there would be colonists suffering from parasites, bacteria or wasp stings showing up here. There was also food poisoning, as practically everything on this planet had to be treated before human consumption. The reverse was generally true, but not always.

Stepping through the big swinging double doors, Ben and Janice entered Dr. Ervin's deserted laboratory. As they strolled through this cavernous room, Ben thought it looked more like some older lab from the Twenty-First Century. Modern Earth hospitals did not normally have sputtering, moving equipment anymore. In Dean's special room were centrifuges spinning, incubators heating, and autoclaves sterilizing. They shined with a pristine metallic finish which looked old, since nothing

21

modern was made of ordinary metal. There was a counter top stretching along the far wall, on which were glass-enclosed chambers, unoccupied by any creature or piece of equipment. There was a box of unpacked plastic beakers by the open office door leading into Dean's office. The hospital still needed a lot of restoration.

Dean was reclining in his chair with the back of his head turned toward them as they entered. His skinny, spidery legs were propped up on a cluttered desktop. He was listening to a small play-back that he held right up to his ear, and began laughing. He looked at the two human shadows altering the rectangular image of the doorway, and turned.

"Hey, hey!" He sprang to his feet. Dressed dark-gray lab jacket, he was almost as tall as Ben, and probably weighed less than a one-fifty. It wasn't enough to call him thin. Dr. Ervin had the body of a human skeleton wrapped in a thin sheath of skin, possessing no fat or muscle that pushed against the wrapping. A scraggly layer of short black hair sat atop his head.

"Just taking a break. I take so much time getting all of these confounded machines running right that it's real inconvenient for me when someone shows up at the door actually needing medical attention."

"Careful, Dean, taking too many breaks will make you appreciate your vacations less," Janice smirked.

Dean winked at her. "Nah. I just take longer vacations." His large eyes shifted up at her husband.

"Hey, Ben, how's your new place coming? Got the AC going?" Ben nodded and offered a smile.

"Our porch is magnificent, but the air conditioner is still in so many little pieces that a surgeon like you would probably have more luck putting it together."

"If you don't mind having pieces left over," Dean answered with a crooked smile. *THIS GUY IS STRANGE!* Ben thought. Most of the medical doctors he had known were anything but jovial and were serious all of the time. They never told jokes and were usually at a loss for any conversation at all. Ben had guessed Dean Ervin's age to be around thirty-five, and like Janice, smiled a lot. Ben had been deliberately holding his hands in his pockets, but now he unconsciously pulled them out. Dean looked down at Ben's thumb and smirked, seeing that it was covered with what looked like dried epoxy. "Problems on the way over here, Ben? You get mugged or something?" Janice offered her classic wrinkled-forehead look.

"Ben got into a wrestling match with one of the flowers. He won –eventually- but needed a weapon do it."

"I am quite certain that this is more than I need to know. Can I offer a mild solvent to remove that little bit of unpleasantness?"

"I'm good. Jan tells me that some serious scrubbing with scouring pad and water will clear it up. Thanks, though."

"Whatever works." Dean walked past them toward the other end of his large office. There was a curtain hanging over the far wall.

"I remember you were telling me you were from Grand Forks? Dakota?"

"North Dakota," Ben answered, trying not to sound like he was correcting him.

"That's seriously arid up there! I'll bet this swimming pool of air is a bit of a shock for you." He took a hard left and rounded a counter top corner, heading toward the drapes. "I'm from Virginia and it still surprised the hell out of me."

"We're adjusting," Ben answered. "I've got a question: what's with the antiques out there?" Dean turned and looked at him.

"Those rickety, chugging, monsters out in the lab? Well, before we left Earth, my boss, Doctor Morahan, and I were given a budget and told to purchase the equipment that we'd need. It was a healthy allotment of funds, enough for some pretty high-tech stuff. But if something like a fancy muon osteograph breaks down, the nearest repair shop is five hundred trillion miles away, so in some cases I purchased older equipment. It's slower, but just as accurate and it was cheap, so I was able to buy two of everything. Plus, if any of it breaks I can fix it myself. I've been servicing these things all morning for the second time just to make sure I have no surprises." Ben nodded. Made sense enough.

Dean stood in front of the curtain. Above it was a hand drawn sign reading: *ERVIN'S MENAGERIE*. He pulled the cloth off to the side, revealing a glass wall behind it, a transparent barricade to another room. This compartment was maybe eight or nine feet each side. Sitting right in the center was a four-legged creature with a blocky,

24

bald head. Its legs were distributed symmetrically around its body. It stood upright was around four feet tall. Its large naked head was larger than Ben's.

"I am host to several natives of Anteros. You probably haven't seen them around, as they prefer to live way above ground in the trees." The head had two dark eyes -black or dark blue- no nose, and a wide mouth that was tightly clamped shut. The forehead was tall, almost conical, and it had a very determined look in the eyes. Its blue skin camouflaged it to blend in with the leaves high up in the trees. Its torso was long and slender, connected with a peculiar four-jointed pelvis that sprang out legs the way that the trunk of a tree shot out its roots.

The harlequin lemur was its name. Each leg had two knee joints, bent at a thirty degree angle as it sat in a resting position with its rear-end suspended a foot off the ground. At the base of each leg was a small foot, from which sprouted long, pencil-thin fingers. The lemur stared at them, appearing as though it were the intellectual observing primitive life forms.

"A perfect example of life on Anteros."

"How so?" Janice asked. Dean leaned over a table and picked up a small sealed test tube with a milky-white, pasty fluid sitting at the bottom. Ben saw the way it sloshed around in the container and clung to the sides like syrup, and knew immediately what it was.

"Blood," Dean said. "Egg-white with a pink tint. We all know at this point that many animals here have white blood, not red. I mean, ours is red

25

because it's a mixture of iron with the oxygen. Hemoglobin in the corpuscles has a chemical structure centered on iron, and when it starts carrying the oxygen, you get a red appearance."

"And because there's so much nickel here, the color of it with oxygen is white, so you get white blood. Ben and I have been studying whenever we've had free time," Jan answered.

"The pink is from some of the proteins it contains, but I haven't identified all of them yet," Dean continued. "I don't know if you knew this, but the harlequin lemur has two separate mouths."

Ben looked surprised. "What? I don't see a second. Is it on the other side of its head?" He looked again. There appeared to be only one, wide enough to reach both sides of its face. The lemur returned the gaze while he observed.

"Mammals on Earth evolved from the sea. Their gills were gradually merged with their alimentary canals -the food slot. We have one opening up top that branches out into the trachea and esophagus, one for air, one for food. This individual evolved with both openings separate and distinct. You can see the mouth for food intake." The lemur kept that mouth closed. It had no lips, so it looked like a thin seam four inches below the eyes. "The other mouth is underneath the chin." Dean said that with a deliberately mischievous tone. Ben looked and saw that he was holding a small one-inch square piece of rubber. He then rubbed it against the glass, making a loud "THUMPTHUMPTHUMPTHUMP!" The quiet lemur hated this, its black eyes bulging to twice

26

their normal size. It propped up on all fours, and a thick flap of muscle and skin dropped down from underneath its chin, revealing a dark, moist pipe. Its throat contorted and made spasmodic, jerking contractions, and then it issued a horrifying hiss. The food mouth, usually closed, hung partly open, revealing bridges of sharp triangular teeth.

"Ben's singing gets the same response out of me," Janice smirked.

"I currently have no patients, so I do this when I'm under-worked and bored," Dean walked back to his desk.

"How intelligent is it?" Janice asked.

"Its brain is enormous. Jan, twenty percent bigger than yours, and probably fifty percent bigger than mine."

"Smart."

"Too smart," Dean replied, losing a small part of his smile.

"What does that mean for us?" she returned.

Dean shrugged." In a thousand years, the harlequin lemurs might be colonizing the Earth, and calling US the lemurs!"

Dean reached down to and picked up the audio recorder, a small device no larger than his thumbnail. His grin was back in full bloom.

"Let's do brunch. But first, I'd like to treat you guys to Hector's most remarkable trait."

"Nice name," Janice said.

"A little overused these days, but why not? Anyhow, I was sitting right on this chair talking into the recorder, with Hector carefully listening to my every word." He pushed the top surface, starting replay.

"**THE IMAGE ENHANCER IS CURRENTLY BROKEN AND I CAN ONLY GUESS AT THE HARLEQUIN LEMUR'S SKELETAL COMPOSITION. ITS DISPOSITION IS CALM AND OBSERVANT, ALWAYS STARING BACK AT ME WITH A SILENT PRIDE, AND I SOMETIMES FEEL AS THOUGH I AM THE ONE IN THE GLASS BOX. AND I SOMETIMES FEEL AS THOUGH I AM THE ONE IN THE GLASS BOX**." It sounded like there had been an echo.

"You repeated yourself," Ben said. Dean shook his head.

"No, I didn't. The lemur was standing right next to me on the other side of the wall, and it repeated what I was saying! It was not only able to mimic my exact words, but my tone of voice perfectly." This is eerie, Ben thought. They started to walk toward the exit. "It must be some kind of a defense instinct, but I have no idea against what. Maybe it uses this talent to distract whatever is trying to prey on it, and it sure weirded me out."

Janice shuddered. "I can't think of anything more disconcerting than my own voice being spoken by an alien," she said. At that moment, her voice emanated from the enclosure,

"**I CAN'T THINK OF ANYTHING MORE DISCONCERTING THAN MY OWN VOICE BEING SPOKEN BY AN ALIEN**." All three stopped and gave the lemur a startled look, which was again quiet. Janice had always had a medium-pitched, sharp voice that carried well, **SOMETIMES TOO WELL**. Ben always found comfort in hearing her words, but now he heard them being spoken by this lemur. He and Janice both looked very uneasy. Creatures like these could wreak all kinds of mischief!

Chapter 2: Pallor

From the hospital they walked to a corner of town, approaching a large wooden building called Koland's, one of a number of restaurants that had recently opened, but this place had the very best food. It was also a general supply store and barber shop. Inside and in the back, behind all of the shelves of canned goods, were half a dozen tables for the people who wished to dine. It was stuffy and dark back there, with windows that were mostly covered over with plant growth.

"I think it's time to make this an outdoor eating establishment." Dean grabbed the edge of a table. "Take the other end, guy, we're moving to the boardwalk." Ben felt awkward, thinking that they should at least get permission from Roger Koland, lest he see them hauling one of his tables out the front door and think he was being robbed. Nothing to worry about, he thought, since I'm the head of law enforcement on Anteros.

They sat around on the wooden walkway, facing the street. Treefall was starting to look like a frontier town, with storefronts sporting big colorful signs advertising hardware or foodstuffs. Several hundred people were outside, high up on ladders hammering away at their shops and houses, working in the yards or just strolling. Welcome to Treefall, the most populated human city on Anteros. Light bikes, those floating motorcycle-shaped hover pods, glistened as they occasionally sped by, the very few luxuries brought from Earth. Kimberly Koland,

Roger's wife, co-owner of the place and hostess appeared in the doorway.

"Hello! It is wonderful to see y'all." She dropped three old-fashioned paper menus at the center of the table. "You just take your time in what you want, now."

"Okay, thanks, Kim," Ben returned, trying not to wince. Kim, since the day she'd left Earth, had always been trying to be a very kind and hospitable woman from somewhere in the Southeastern United states, even though it was painfully obvious to every human being on this world (and probably most of the animals here) that she was really from New Hampshire.

Dean pulled something out of his front pocket.

"Why wait, let's eat now." He dropped a small gray bar on the table. Janice picked it up, still surprised by the density.

"I can't believe that everything we're about to ask for is going to come from a five-inch-long block of chemicals."

"Correction, four inches of chemicals, four-by-one-by-a-half-inch, to make any dish you want. In here is every single element that humans need to live on -carbon, phosphorous -anything- and we can use this to make whatever we wish for, just add water, of which we have way too much here, and a food processor. Just plug it in, drop a few of these in, and you could have anything from devilled eggs to chicken kiev!"

"Don't remind me." Ben said. "We have a ten-year supply of these things in those four warehouses in the center of town. One of my first tasks after we

31

got everything offloaded from the landers was to visually verify that something like two-hundred million of these food bars were actually there." Ben picked it up. It was very heavy for the size. "These really are a technological miracle that will keep us alive, but only after a lot of work. It may use ideal animal and plant DNA to manufacture the materials, but it's not like you can program the machine to even make a loaf of bread, because they only clone the raw ingredients, like chicken muscle, grains or onions. We were surprised at how much effort is needed in prepping everything."

"We have the standard TN-Nine that was issued to us, but, I mean this technology is just so new. It isn't like everyone in the country back home had one, because they were too expensive. Ben and I read an instruction manual for the first time when we were trying to make ourselves dinner on our first night on here." Janice continued. "We put in five food cards and got out a massive slab of raw beef muscle and a head of lettuce. We tried to program it to generate some spices, but what came out smelled genuinely toxic, so out they went. Our dinner that night was a couple of humongous steaks we had intended to be top sirloin, but literally tasted like rubber after the grill," she looked at Ben. "No offense."

"None taken, it's well deserved."

"And we had all of this dried-out lettuce with no dressing, so suffice it to say, our first meal was dreadful. The next day, the lunch was awful, too."

"We eat out a lot," Ben continued.

"What about when you were back on Earth?" Dean inquired with a smile, knowing the answer.

"There, too. Janice and I both were definitely a work-in-progress as far as home-cooked meals go."

"That's my husband's euphemism for us being absolutely abominable at cooking." She looked at Ben, who was smiling widely. "I know you're aching to tell the last fiasco we had back home, so go for it." Ben loved this.

"Six months before we left to go here, Janice decided that she was going to bake a start-from-scratch, World's Greatest Lasagna." He started laughing." I'm sorry, but I can never tell this with a straight face. Anyhow, I had to do some OT that day, but when I came home, I saw that she had basically destroyed our kitchen. She was wearing about a third of the ingredients, although tomato sauce in her hair was a perfect match. The only thing missing was a mushroom cloud hovering over her head. You really had to see it, and I just stood there trying not to laugh, but still did, while Janice is standing in the middle of this wasteland, clearly pissed off, and staring at me with her patented 'What?' look. Anyhow, she'd gotten the calamity into the oven and two hours later we had our romantic dinner. If we had been a family of twelve there still would have been enough, but this particular meal was kind of interesting in that it needed a jackhammer to soften it up. I'm glad we had some wine there to make things a little easier." He looked at Jan, who was enjoying it all. "Please continue with the second half."

She joyously did. "A week later, when Ben had Saturday off, he figured he'd show me up and make a true New England Clam-Chowder from square-one. Whatever horror that he'd hallucinated would be masterpiece chowder was so hideous that it'd had made my first attempt at Italian seem delicious! We got about one, maybe two spoon-fulls into this atrocity -make that one- when he looks at me and says, 'Hey, we've been wanting to try that new Jo Ling's place, so let's go now. Please, let's just go now,' and in spite of Ben's wonderful dinner that almost needed a haz-mat team to clean up after, we actually had a nice meal of some genuinely authentic Chinese cuisine." Ben looked very seriously at Dean.

"So, we eat out a lot."

Kim now returned, and they all ordered. Janice's had caught all of their attention, though, with what she wanted.

"I believe in healthy eating, so I'll go with the full salad with olives and tomatoes, but also with a double serving of ranch dressing. And bacon bits – make that bacon chunks, I'd also like that too, please." And now Ben gave his very rare roll-of-the-eyes.

"Damn, Janice, would you like them toss some onion rings on top of all that healthy salad, just to make sure you live at least a hundred more years?" he asked. Janice turned to him and returned her daily caustic look.

"Absolutely."

They savored lunch, eating slowly and learning more about one another's lives. There was a full moon out, Pallor, a huge red circular circle against the bluish-purple sky. All three of them gazed up.

"Just like Mars," Dean said, not looking away. It was dark and covered with sulfurous volcanos.

"More like Io, with that bloody-looking surface and all of those black holes. Nasty," Ben said. From arm's reach, Earth's moon would have been a golf ball and Pallor a basketball. Like Mars it had a thin carbon dioxide atmosphere, but this Anteran satellite didn't have polar caps, it was too warm to freeze CO_2.

"Pallor," Ben said. "Interesting name." He didn't have any idea where it came from, but he had an idea that Dean did, and would probably....

"Terror," Dean answered. "The moon is terror, in more ways than one."

Janice sat up. "I thought 'Palla' meant pale."

"Pale with fear." Dean looked at both of them. "The Greek god Mars had five special attendants, cheery fellows like Phobos, Deimos, Pallor, Eris, and Metus. These people had embodied the traits associated with war, an activity to which Mars was partial. Some professional Greek mythologist back in Washington D.C. decided to name this moon Pallor."

"You've done your homework," Janice remarked.

"You have to in a place like this, since there's so much danger, as the original settlers in this town found out. We're called surveyors, sent here before the thousands of colonists because it's our job, all of us, to identify the many nasty ways you can die on Anteros."

"You're such an optimist," Janice replied.

"And it's my business to keep you dreamy-eyed explorers from prancing off into the daisies and getting eaten," Ben said. Dean looked at him and grinned.

"That's right, what's the actual title, the sheriff?" Ben had never really cared for that term. It was a little too rustic-sounding for this big city kid.

"Nah. I'm the Chief Safety Officer. You see, the last I'd heard up until a two months ago on that transport, was that I was to be the deputy assistant of CSO Kevin Hedrick. Well, light only travels so fast, and the only way faster are those extremely expensive interstellar ships that seem to only want to unload people and cargo as quick as possible and leave. Anyhow, we were told that Hedrick had not been seen for a couple years, and his deputy left on the ship that had brought us all here, telling me that I was now the acting chief, but that was about it. I mean, I'd been a mid-level officer back in Grand Forks, and originally designated to be a second-in-command in a four-man safety force, but now I'm in charge of the safety office with one assistant. There was supposed to be a town council that was actually functional, some elected governor, or mayor or something, and everyone else on our ship thought the same, but there just wasn't. So I'm here trying to figure out how to keep over five-hundred people alive, and what's happened to the others. But really, I don't like to be called safety officer, or chief safety officer. Anyone who knows me calls me Ben. I'd appreciate that."

Dean nodded. "This has to be a lot of unanticipated responsibility for you, and I think you'll get everything resolved, including this last person who isn't in town anymore. Is that the kind of work you did back in Grand Forks?"

"I was with the Grand Forks Police Department for twenty years, working most of the time as a kind of informal department machine-builder and drone-operator. I was field certified, so sometimes I would get farmed out to other divisions –missing persons for three years, and before that two in larceny."

"Ben and I met because he was working in the theft division and was investigating my roommate's stolen car," Janice continued. Ben reached over and they joined hands.

"For most of the time I was just kind of working with gadgets, improving scopes, that kind of thing. Janice had been accepted for her current position here, so I took an early retirement." *IT SURE WAS AN EARLY RETIREMENT!*

"What brought you to join the police?"

"Well, I majored in electrical engineering in college, specialized in film electronics, like those in house windows and car windshields that show you speed limits and signs, you know?"

"A little, I've read about it some."

"Anyhow, it was a terrible market for engineers when I graduated, so I went through the basic training program for the Grand Forks Police Department. Man, they loved me. They were really looking for technical people, especially folks who knew how to manipulate electrons and make them move from one point to another." Ben's smile of

37

reminiscence faded a little. He had grown to hate that job in Grand Forks, everything about it. "I mainly worked in counter terrorist SWAT, a little group of two dozen people whose job it was to locate threats."

"What kind of threats?"

"Explosives, chemical agents, biological weapons, all the tricks of the trade."

Dean shook his head. "I never could understand that. Fanatics who see things only through a very narrow corridor, and feel that anyone outside this field, involved or not, innocent or not, must be an enemy and killed."

"There were a lot of causes, but my job was to just locate the bombs. We left the motives for people in intelligence."

"How did you locate them?"

"I still can't talk about it." Ben saw the blank look on Dean's face. "I know you're not one of the bad guys, and that no one here is, but it's just that when you work in that profession, you really get used to not talking about anything being investigated. Even when it's declassified, you just don't speak a word of it." Dean looked at Janice, who was unusually somber. She was a veteran, too. "The terrorists employed listening devices, sometimes bugs the size of molecules to spy on us. Some were designed to look just like house flies or gnats. That's why we didn't talk about technical specifics even among ourselves in secure areas. I'm serious, a guy can get real paranoid when working in counter-terrorism."

Dean sighed grimly. "Terrorism is a horrific political expression that is only getting more intense." He was referring to their home country, the North American States.

"That," Janice said, "is four hundred light years west of here. It's why I grabbed the first chance I could to get off the Earth and start over somewhere else."

Dean smiled at her. "How's the Smithsonian?" Janice nodded. "I've been with the Smithsonian Tropical Research Institute for my entire career, before I even had my doctorate, and interned there every summer since my senior year. In Grand Forks, I was a botanist confined to our apartment, working on a computer. I would go off to Costa Rica or the Amazon Reserves once or twice a year, but those rain forests are so small now, it was more depressing than educational. And I was never allowed to stay there long enough."

"She'd arranged for our honeymoon down in Costa Rica," Ben added. Dean chortled. He looked down the road toward the edge of town, where the thick trees and vines towered up a thousand yards away.

"I myself was on a waiting list to tour the Costa Rican reserves," he said.

"And how long was the wait?" Janice asked, knowing the answer. To pay for tuition during her senior year in college, she had been a tour guide down in Costa Rica. Real Neotropical rain forests were some of the rarest things on Earth.

"Fifteen years. Millions of people want just a taste of what a real forest is like. Then one of my colleagues at the University of Virginia told me they were looking for an assistant general surgeon and internist, both of which happen to be my specialties, to fly off to Anteros on a survey. A preliminary description said it was hot and had a lot of trees. It sounded kind of fun, so I applied. I was competing against about a thousand other physicians for the job. No kidding, a thousand. I didn't think I had a prayer, but next thing I knew I was putting my 500th floor condo on the market and packing my bags."

"Not like any reservation back home, eh?" Janice smirked.

"These are the real tropics. Alien, with strange insects and birds and snakes. I don't mind telling you that I'm more than a little frightened, especially with all of those people from the last survey gone that you're currently investigating." Dean said. Janice agreed with a nod.

"I'll figure it out," Ben answered.

They finished brunch, the best yet, and walked down the wooden sidewalk, and Dean was looking straight up, entranced. One foot slipped off the wooden walkway and sank into the muddy street. He pulled it back without taking his eyes off the sky.

"You have a clear view of the other moon," Dean said, "Eris." They stopped. From behind the crimson face of Pallor, there emerged the second moon orbiting Anteros. It wasn't a circle in the sky, or even remotely spherical in shape.

"Wow," Janice said staring up, her jaw pulling down.

"I've never seen it this close." Eris was a craggy corpse of what was once a good-sized moon. Five-hundred million years ago something massive had hurled itself into it. It hadn't merely left a crater, it destroyed the moon completely. A comet or third moon had smashed into it with such a velocity that half of the surface of Eris all the way down to its deepest insides had been blown completely away.

"Cr-r-razy sky!" Dean said. He sounded very strange, but Ben was starting to get used to this.

"What?" he asked.

"Crazy sky. You haven't heard that?" Ben and Janice shook their heads. "Have you heard of an event called the two-year terror?"

"Very definitely," Ben answered. "Every two years the whole planet, especially around the equator, goes really nuts. This is one of the few things we all knew before landing." Treefall was located on a great northern continent, a thousand miles inland from a very dangerous ocean, so it was shielded from the worst aspects of the two-year ordeal. Dean had done some serious background on this.

"Twenty-eight years ago, the geologists who'd first surveyed this planet sent a message from the surface back to their mother ship. Just before the occurrence of what came to be called this cataclysm, their report described the sky as being filled with huge asteroids moving into plain view, extremely big rocks. Their communication stated that these flew within a few hundred miles of Anteros, that asteroid belt orbiting Anteros, with

41

Eris right in the middle of it. Whatever had struck it so many eons ago scattered its remains everywhere, and there are some very deep and wide impact craters on Anteros as a reminder. The last recording that the commander of the survey group made from the surface to the orbiter mentioned a 'crazy sky.' After that they were hit by the terror."

Dean started walking again, this time very fast with a destination in mind.

"Let's take a look at the Vanguard Memorial. I think that we need a second statue for the people of the Second Survey who died here, though. We know this place at least a little better, and hopefully there won't need to be a third one for us." Dean said.

"There will be another site to recognize the Second, Dean, as soon as Treefall pulls itself together, elects a town council and makes some resources available for it. And we won't have a third, because we're going to learn about how to live here," Ben answered. There was a great monument in the town that had a simple octagonal base of granite, and mounted by metal fixtures. They'd been deliberately distorted, but if you stared at these glittering objects long enough, they appeared to be a hand-held compass and a plumb bob. Placed proudly on the base was a silvery plaque captioned, "WE REMEMBER." Ben read on.

WE REMEMBER

The fifty-four men and women of the First Anteran Survey Expedition, who perished while forging this new home for Humanity. We shall never forget their sacrifice.

The First Anteran Survey, assigned by United States Astro-Space Reconnaissance, had visited this world after a five-year voyage in deep sleep. When they awoke in orbit around the planet, they first noticed those two incredible suns, the brilliant Orpheus orbiting very closely around the huge but stable red subgiant Eurydice. Orpheus was much smaller than its neighbor, but so much brighter. From this distance these two suns looked frightfully close together, with their white and red hues blending and filling in the gap between them. And then they looked down at the new planet. From their high geosynchronous orbit they observed a ring of land that wrapped completely around the planet's equator, about five-hundred miles wide. It was mountainous and brown and totally lifeless. North of this strange continent was a second ring, this one a blue ocean, that also formed an uninterrupted circle around this world. Above this thousand-mile-wide body of water was more land, which extended all the way up to the pole. This was a massive polar continent was peppered with millions of lakes, the largest being the size of the Black Sea. Nothing was frozen. South of the equatorial continent was a second ocean that encircled the planet, this one extending about half-way down to the south pole, touching on a hemispherical continent similar to the one in the north.

They were under the command of Colonel Jason Curtis of U.S.A.S.R., happily married and father of two daughters, both of whom had graduated college right before he'd left, and were pursuing very different fields, one in late seventeenth century early American literature and the other in nucleon fusion generator tech. One had always called him "Dad," and the other "Papa Jay." Sibling rivalry, he'd muse, even between twins. They were never one person, had always competed against each other to be their own, and each of them won. They both cried when he greeted them at the departure terminal, but he assured,

"I'll be back in ten years –just a wink for you two youngsters. I've been in this field for my entire life, and this is something I have to do, but know that I love you both and will always be thinking about you."

His friends back at ASR-Denver had humorously dubbed him the "Poet Astronaut," a nickname that stuck with him for his entire thirty-year career. He had a doctorate in geology and found this incredible new star system to be "Mead for my mind and a song for my soul, a true dream job." It had been decided some decades earlier to name this new-found world after relations of the Mars. It was Anteros, God of Passion, son of Mars and Venus.

Equipped with four landers (hopper craft), the survey team had broken up into two groups, both of them landing on the middle continent. The first touched ground close to sea level, at the tip on a long, narrow fjord jutting up two hundred miles into the northern ocean. The second, led by Colonel Curtis, landed high up in the alpine regions. Here the shield volcanoes and mountains rose up from

44

the oceanic crust and towered up into the sky, ten miles above sea level in some areas. This place (later named the Oreade Mountains) was never completely cool. Over their long history these volcanos had violently erupted, building up the surrounding range until it was so high that it sank back into the ocean crust under its own weight. Today they looked a bit menacing, but all of the instrument readings showed that the underlying magma pockets were stable. There was also a non-stop rumbling underneath the ground -an earthquake which neither diminished nor grew.

It was midday, but the sky was strange, peppered with large, dark objects. Before landing, they had observed a huge moon in a very close orbit. Anteros was a binary planetary system, not a sphere with a lone dependent, like Earth was. This gigantic-sized satellite, Harmonia, was on the other side of the planet and could not be seen. But they did see the mysterious second moon, Enyo, a jagged, blocky-looking chunk of rock, swiftly moving overhead. This ugly satellite had serrated corners poking out into space. Beyond these was a valley that dropped all the way down to the core of the moon itself. Some celestial collision had shattered this small world, and what was left was maybe half the size of Earth's moon. But it was coming in so close! Curtis spoke into a recorder, sending a message back to the automated mother ship:

"Enyo died a horrific death countless years ago. I look at it and the level of destruction, unchanged over the years by any erosion, and I believe that it is the most violent symbol I have ever beheld. I can see parts of it all over the sky, many of them fragments large enough to eclipse the two suns for some seconds, as clouds do when they pass overhead. Some of these asteroids bolt across the heavens with astonishing rapidity, while others seem to just sit up in the sky motionless. This is truly a crazy sky."

Anteros had gotten used to the steady tug of its nearer moon Harmonia. But every two years Enyo would pass very close to the world on the opposite side. Now it moved over the first human beings here, covering them in darkness. This event seemed to drop the hammer on a loaded gun cocked beneath the crust of this world. An intense earthquake suddenly hit them. The underlying plates were a taut rubber band that had snapped. The shaking of the ground had been holding a continuous 4.4 on the Richter scale when they landed, but now it suddenly increased. The scale went from 4.4 to 7.0 in seconds, and then jumped to 8.0 and then 9.0. The survey group suddenly found themselves in a 9.9 earthquake. There were no buildings or trees to come crashing down on them, but the heaving ground threw them off their feet and hammered against them. They floundered on the surface, slowly beaten to death by its vibrations. Then Colonel Curtis saw with horror that twelve of his crew, as they writhed helplessly on the ground, began screaming in agony. Beneath them the surface itself boiled. Rocks heated and glowed, and their clothes and skin and hair caught fire. A magma pocket suddenly opened up beneath them, and a second later they were gone -incinerated in a fiery explosion. A new volcano was born with a spray of fresh lava. Twenty survivors scampered desperately toward their hopper craft, which so far had withstood the violent shaking without tipping over. But the ground not only moved in an up-and-down motion, it shifted from side-to-side as well. It was like crawling on a very slippery floor and they got nowhere. Lava teemed out of the incipient vent and rolled toward the helpless explorers. It was moving one or two feet per second. With but a fast walk someone could have escaped from its path, BUT THESE PEOPLE COULDN'T MOVE! They were helpless against the pummeling. They scrambled against the ground to no avail as their fate slowly rolled up and enveloped them one by one. Their ship was only a few feet away, and remained so for the rest of their lives.

Three-hundred miles away, the sea group had lost communications with Curtis. The shaking was not as bad in their area --maybe a 6.0, but they were able to remain standing and their hoppers had not been damaged. The huge mountain range to the south had suddenly become immersed in a rainstorm of red lava. They immediately decided to fly to Curtis's group to provide a possible rescue lift. They looked toward the ocean and were terrified to see that a wall of water, a tidal wave thousands of feet high, was roaring towards them. It stretched as far as they could see in both directions, and looked as though it was swallowing the whole planet! Before they could reach their hoppers, they were blown to pieces by the momentum of the wave.

Ever since the nightmarish lesson learned by the ASR, the name of the wounded, scarred moon that had caused this every two years had been changed. It was renamed Eris, the embodiment of discord. Harmonia was renamed Pallor, the embodiment of terror. Every couple of years, terror and discord tried to tear Anteros apart, an event known as the Two-Year Terror. Janice and Ben left town and took a different, much more bending trail home, quickly becoming engulfed in the shadow of canopy branches. They walked quietly for five minutes, staring up at the pinnacles, when they came upon a different tree called a honey willow. It sat in its own little clearing and looked like a tall stack of enormous white umbrellas three hundred feet tall. Branches sprouted from the trunk at the hundred foot mark, and they quickly subdivided further into long, stringy stalks of elastic wood that drooped beneath their weight. But the tree looked hazy, as though in a rainstorm. As they approached, Ben noticed that he couldn't see the trunk. The honey willow did not bear fruit; rather, its thin branches drooled, secreting very light-weight, cobweb-like strings of honey, pollen and fructose that dangled to the ground. Millions of these hung like pendulums, totally masking the tree's central column. There was one branch that stood out and away from the rest, dripping a solitary honey vine. Janice suddenly halted at this line.

"Stop here, Ben. Five feet from the outer branches is the closest anyone should get." Ben reached toward the outer the strand, so thin he could barely see it. With just a touch the hundred-and-fifty-foot-long string came spiraling down. It was light, almost floating on air, so he and Janice had time to step out of the way before becoming drenched in honey. Ben looked at his finger, coated with the goopy, yellow film.

"Taste it," Janice said. Ben gave Janice a disbelieving squint. "Really. There's no poison or nickel content in it, just sugar and carbonaceous seeds." She gave a proud smile. "I recently completed a small report about the honey willow tree."

"It looks like something out of a fairytale," Ben dunked his finger into his mouth and thoroughly cleaned it. It was sweet enough to bring tears to his eyes. He had never tasted anything like this, the most sugar-laden cake not even coming close. "It's good," His voice crackled and his throat was tickled by the rush of sugar. Janice grinned and nodded, but then her expression turned gravely serious. She didn't show this look often and could seize Ben's attention whenever she did.

"Never go inside the honey willow, Ben. I'm even a little uncomfortable standing this close to it. We're safe just pulling off some enticements, just stay out."

"Why? What's in there?" Janice didn't answer. She listened carefully for ten seconds.

"Hear that?" she asked. Ben listened. He never had a trained ear for listening to the rain forest, but he heard a faint, low-pitched droning sound. Only one kind of insect could make a buzzing noise like that.

"Honey wasps," she continued. "They nest all along the trunk, and never leave the confines of the willow. Their entire society is structured solely around this tree. Animals and people who go just around the edges will just track pollen around. But when some happy-go-lucky creature gets a little too greedy and penetrates too deeply into it, it never comes out. The wasps, as far as people know, are carnivores, and they're not alone in there." She stooped down and felt the ground, inviting Ben with her eyes to do the same. He could feel it vibrating.

"Feels like --"

"Footsteps, thousands of them," Janice continued. There are some other animals living in there. No one knows what they are, but they're there, generating all these footfalls that we can feel. I sent two drones in there a few weeks ago, and they stopped communicating before they could send back a single image." She stood up, still looking very sober. "So just keep your distance from the honey willow, Ben."

"Always," Ben answered. Janice smiled again. She knew her field, he thought, and he was very certain that he'd perish on this world without her.

Chapter 3: Janice

A month after Ben turned twenty-eight, SWAT had loaned him to the Grand Forks General Operations and Larceny Department. This temporary job wasn't as exciting as counter-terrorism, and he was thankful for that. When working for SWAT four years earlier, he'd experienced the most traumatic physical and emotional injury of his life. It was followed by months of rehabilitative therapy, a department commendation which neither he nor anyone else in the division had felt he deserved, and a very ugly scar.

General Ops still kept him very busy. He hadn't logged those kinds of hours since his second year on the force, and spent half of his time near the college campus, Stenman University. One Friday in the middle of the spring semester, Ben pulled up in front of Mittler Apartments in his sand-colored police car, and emerged wearing his usual light tan desert camo police uniform. It was late, and the walkways were jammed with students giving him a long stare. Something was up.

The university was a huge institution that offered degrees mostly in biological and life sciences. It was hard to get accepted into this place, but the more dedicated a school professes to be, he thought, the more trouble its students get into. He had graduated from a rival college across town some six years earlier, but it still felt like yesterday. He approached Mittler, a twenty-story tower that had hosted mostly upper-classman students and people who were just starting out. Dozens of people were sitting on the grass studying. A Frisbee tournament was taking place on the yard, with athletes running vigorously, and doing a talented tap dance around the seated people when required. A group of ten whooping, screaming students stampeded past Ben, all piling through the front doorway at once. A long banner, starting from the tenth floor and hanging down to the fourth, read: **HERES THE PARTY!!!!** Ben threw his head back, read it, and laughed. Several people stopped in their tracks and smiled at him. He might have been a police officer, but at least he wasn't there to break up their fun! His destination was on the fourteenth floor.

The tall and thin plastic door was manually pushed to the side by the occupant. She was twenty-one or twenty-two years old, and unbelievably beautiful, standing at five foot seven and possessing long, perfectly straight blond hair, not a stray one in the lot. Her face was immaculate and she had glowing red cheeks, with bright mascara changing to a dark tan around her intensely blue eyes. Her teeth were bright white, with an artificial thin line of gold along the front of the crowns. She was fully electrified tonight, and smiled brightly.

"Hi! I'm Donna Baylor, Officer Porterfield." She had her eyes transfixed momentarily on his tag. "Are you here about my car?" Ben returned the smile.

"Yes."

"Come in." She led him into the large living room. It was cluttered with several folding tables

52

and four computers on the floor, along with a thousand sheets of hard copies which could almost be called a wall-to-wall carpet. Sitting cross-legged on the floor was a rather ordinary looking woman, probably the same age as Donna. Her face was plain and white, with no electronically-deposited make-up changing and contorting it. She was hunched over studying a fifth computer screen intensely.

"This is my roommate, Janny Gifford." Janice looked up. Her red hair was long and the bangs drooped a completely over her eyes. She gave him a weird smile, stretching her mouth back on the right side of her face. "The pad wart," Donna continued. Janny kept her smile and gave her a sarcastic nod, and looked back down on the screen. This obscure girl appeared to be the exact opposite of her roommate, dressed in a pair of rolled up Bermuda shorts and an old train operator's jacket, maybe five sizes too big for her.

"Sorry about the mess," Donna said. "Midterms."

"Been there."

"Been where?"

"North Dakota State, Grand Forks," Ben answered. Donna brightened.

"Ahhh, our inimical foes from yonder suburbia." She picked up a pencil-sized rod and walked into the small bathroom, standing in front of the mirror and studying herself with the same resolution as Janny did her computer. She fiddled with several small buttons on the end of the tubular gadget without even looking -a veteran- and held it up to her face. The red on her left cheek almost magically changed from bright pink to violet to a dark purple. She repeated this procedure for the other side.

"You're here about the theft, right? To get my side of the story?" she asked, not taking her eyes off of her reflection.

"Yeah. We have a statement from Thomas Grant, Boyfriend."

"Ex-boyfriend. I ex'd him two weeks ago," Donna coldly answered.

"Go on." She turned. Now she had changed the color around her eyes and it was almost pitch black.

"I got a call on Wednesday night, at eight-o-five, to be exact, from Thomas. The jerk calls me from his phone in my own car, and tells me that he's gonna drive it to Southard Park and put it in the fountain. Janny was here."

"I was here," Janice mumbled, totally uninterested."

"From my own car! What an asshole! He's not what you'd call bright, though. He called me just as he was leaving the parking lot down below, and I just happened to be standing by the window when I saw my car being stolen."

"What kind was it?"

"A twenty-five, metallic green Oslo Motors Skoll II coup, two hundred kilowatts. I tell Janice, 'he's right down there! He's rubbing my nose in this and thinks there's nothing I can do!'"

"What did you do?"

"I opened the window and threw a cactus at him." Ben was staring at the blinking light on his recorder, holding his breath. If he exhaled, he would

54

giggle. He looked up and saw that Janice was staring at him, smiling with that odd grin. *Go ahead*, she silently urged, *laugh at her. That's what I've been doing for the last two days!* Ben was barely able to hold it in. He forced a serious expression onto his face that must have looked hideous. He fought his tickled throat muscles and asked,

"Cactus?"

"A little baby cactus growing in a flowerpot. I threw the whole thing at him, too, -pot, dirt, and cactus."

"I guess it's lucky you didn't have a pet cat handy," Ben answered. He heard laughing from Janice's side of room."

"Anyhow, the pot landed on the hood of my car, bounced off and sent dirt and cactus parts flying everywhere. Then I reported it to you cops, and got a call back five minutes later saying you guys had caught him." Ben stood there nodding. "That's my story. When do I get my car back?"

"Monday."

"He didn't get it into the fountain, did he?"

"Never even got onto the grass. By the way, don't throw anything out of that window again, public endangerment laws and all, okay?"

"Got it."

Ben turned to Janice. "Do you have anything to add to this?" Janice looked up.

"It was my cactus." Ben smiled and turned back to Donna.

"I guess the big question is, what do you want to do about Mister Grant?"

"I want to file a Grand Forks LC-14 Pre-indictment Form." Ben stared at her. She had done her homework.

"You want him charged with grand larceny?" Then she asked a question that he hated to hear.

"Well, what do you think I should do?" Ben paused for a long moment. He knew that Janice, although pretending to mind her own business, was acutely absorbing every word they said.

"It's really your call. What kind of person is Mister Grant?"

"He's a car stealing bastard!"

"I mean before he was an alleged car stealing bastard." The grotesque black rings around her eyes masked all her feelings. She stared at the floor for several seconds.

"He is totally irresponsible. He's big and good looking, so he doesn't have a problem with women, know what I mean? He doesn't have much competition, so he doesn't have to grow up."

"Is he violent? Dangerous or abusive?"

"Oh, hell no."

"I checked his record and he's pretty clean-cut. Is he okay?"

"Except for that one time, yeah."

Ben smiled. "Just went off the deep end that night?" Donna nodded. "Well, if you charge him and he eventually gets convicted, it's the kind of thing that will probably mess him up badly. After jail he'll have an extremely nasty criminal record for the rest of his life. You want my opinion? Well, he didn't hurt anyone, and didn't try to. He just did something pretty damn stupid. Just something for you to think about, so get back to me about what action you want to take." Donna stood there for a moment before saying,

"I'll be merciful and let the moron walk. But I want you to yell at him for a while before letting him go." Ben smiled and nodded.

"Okay, I guess that's everything I need." He turned and started for the door when Donna's mysterious roommate called out,

"Hey! What was your major?"

"What? Thin film electrical engineering, class of twenty," Ben answered. "Janny" jumped up and rushed over to him, clutching her computer.

"Ever take the gravity class?" She asked. *THE INFAMOUS GRAVITY CLASS FROM HELL,* Ben thought.

"Yeah." Janice moved up right beside him and stuck the white screen display in his face.

"Have I got something for you!" The display had a paragraph at the top, and a schematic of several boxes below it. "The question starts with three connected rooms, as seen in Figure 3-1. They are each connected with a three foot by six foot doorway. Assuming some 'magical' gravitic generator is underneath the central room, they want us to derive the gravitic flux that'll give 1-G on the floor, and 0.5-G's along the walls and ceiling. Assume that all corners have a radius of two inches." Ben remembered having that same homework problem seven years ago, the hardest science problem in the world, and it took ten excruciating hours to finally figure it out. But when that exact question surfaced on his mid-term, he'd forgotten it!"

"What do you want to know?" he asked. Janny stared up at him.

"The function! The math that gives the function -anything!" She looked at the screen for several more seconds and then up into his eyes. Donna's voice suddenly bellowed from across the room as she marched toward the door.

"You pad warts make me sick!"

"Good," Janice snapped, her eyes still fixed on his.

"It's Friday and I'm going out." Donna left them alone. Janice smiled out of the corner of her mouth.

"Thank God." She looked back down at the computer. "This question is so stupid. It simply states that there's some crazy generator spewing out artificial gravity. You're an engineer, how is something like this really done?"

"Not with one unit. Gravity engineers line the floor and walls with circuits. They're a lot like electrical boards, but instead of moving electrons and sending out magnetic waves, they generate and push around gravitons. It's incredible! There are gravitic capacitors, inductors, diodes -everything comparable to an electrical unit, embedded in Teflon pads that are as thin as paper."

"What about the 0.5 G's on the walls? Does anyone actually do that?"

"Nah. The prof's just making it hard."

"So, give me some hints!" Ben felt a little embarrassed.

"I don't remember," he said. "It's difficult, I know that. Want some advice?"

"Please."

"Just go through the text. Study like mad, bug your professor for help, do whatever it takes to learn it." Janice set the pad down on a table and looked at him.

"I'm not even planning to be an engineer. I'm just taking this class because, according to Donna, the Evil Fairy Princess, I'm a masochistic pad wart."

"What's your major?" Ben asked.

"I'm almost done with my third year and I'm still undecided. It's going to be either something in botany or biology. I've taken a lot of classes in each."

"What's with the gravity class?" Ben asked. Janice gave him a nonchalant shrug.

"We're required to take some pretty general physical science electives. I already took this last fall, thinking all we'd learn is why things don't just float off the Earth. Ha! We finished with that in the first half hour. I took an impact that semester, to be sure. Did great in everything except gravity class, which I failed. So I'm taking it again."

"Why?"

"Because I just don't like the idea of taking a defeat like that and moving on. I'll keep repeating it If I have to, but I will learn the gravity course, even if I never use it." He stared into her eyes for five seconds before becoming embarrassed. This slovenly, unseen roommate of the ever-fashionable Donna Baylor was fascinating, and he felt an enormously strong admiration for her that he knew

59

would never subside. He reached down into his shirt pocket, realizing he'd forgotten to turn off the recorder. He moved toward the door, but "Janny" (Ben found out later that she hated that nickname with a passion) stood still. He stepped toward her and extended his hand.

"It was nice talking with you, Janice. Good luck with your class." Janice shook it and smiled.

"Take care," she said, corner-smiling. Ben left.

WHAT SHOULD I DO? He asked himself the next day. He was haunted with possible actions he might take that could be entirely inappropriate: a uniformed Grand Forks police officer asking out the roommate of a woman who had been a victim of grand larceny! The theft was more comical than anything else, but he was still worried about making an ass out of himself. Janice Gifford with the strange smile, the diehard gravity student who dressed the part of both a beach bum and a train engineer. He couldn't erase her image, and beyond that two-dimensional picture was positively a third dimension of a truly amazing personality. Now he sent her a message:

FROM: BENJAMIN PORTERFIELD
TO: JANICE GIFFORD

I PERSONALLY ENJOYED TALKING WITH YOU. WOULD YOU LIKE TO GO TO THE SUTTON TREE RESERVE WITH ME ON SATURDAY?

And then came that horrible half-day wait with no response. She might have been out, he told himself. He hoped this was it, but Ben also suspected that Janice Gifford had a line of prospective boyfriends, and that he was at the end of it. The happiest moment in his life came at two o'clock in the morning when his phone lit up:

FROM: JANICE GIFFORD
TO: BENJAMIN PORTERFIELD
DEFINITELY!

Chapter 4: The Willow

On the morning after the encounter with the honey tree, Ben sat in a wicker chair in the corner of the bedroom, folding up his pants sleeves up a little to avoid dragging around fifty pounds of clinging mud all day. *I LOOK PRETTY RIDICULOUS*, he thought, and this shirt was anything but discrete. It was a size too small, pressed against his sides and advertised in large white letters printed on the back,

SAFETY OFFICER
BENJAMIN PORTERFIELD

He felt like a little kid wearing a T-shirt reading:

HI! MY NAME IS BEN!

Janice was having a little more trouble getting motivated to get up for work, always being a hopeless slob before eight. She rolled over and looked at her husband.

"Stylish clothes," she said with a waking mumble, "when I was a kid I used to beat up boys for dressing like you." Ben smirked and buttoned up his shirt. "I'll bet you never thought I'd drag you off to Anteros. You said it wouldn't happen, but here we are." Ben stood up and smiled at her. "We're quite a twosome -a Grand Forks policeman, and a Neotropical ecologist. I'm glad we got off, Ben, and that Earth is out of reach." He looked into her hazels.

"Want to know something surprising? So am I."

"That is surprising."

"Earth just seems to be getting a little too, hell, casual, I guess. It's trendy for people to simply say, 'it's time to spread out' and divorce every few years. It's even a status symbol to have been married five or more times. I kind of like the idea of us being way off the trail. It means we're stuck with each other." Janice stared at him very seriously, propping her head up on her arm.

"We've been married for many years, my love. But even back in the city, the thought of ever being away from you just never occurred to me."

"Get ready for a shock, Janice. You hauled me out here to a planet that's years from Earth, so now you're gonna have to put up with me for five or six more decades."

"Wow, that's fifty or sixty years."

"You got it."

"That's a life to me and I like it." Ben examined the 4.25 pistol and then the stunner and clamped his mouth down hard. "You worked for twenty years in the force, but retired without giving me a lot of argument, just so we could move here. Why?"

"It's not a big deal."

"I know that you had some problems in Grand Forks, but I also know you loved the place. The people, the, open areas outside of town, everything about home. Do you think about it a lot?"

"You know, I was really ready to move on, and wanted to. But when I came home that Tuesday and saw your hysterical smile and nutsy eyes glowing as you told me you had been asked to participate on the Third Anteran Survey, it wouldn't have mattered. If I'd been the police commissioner, about ready to win the governor's race, I would have quit that to go with you, because I want you to revel in a life you've always wanted, and it really brings a happiness to me that I wouldn't know if I wasn't part of yours, because I'd be just be desolate without you."

"But do you feel like I coaxed you into this? That I would have gone to Anteros without you? This is actually pretty important for me to know."

"I absolutely do not. As a matter of fact, I feel like I'm a tag-a-long husband, someone who never would have been even considered to be part of this Anteran Expedition had I not been married to someone who was indispensable to it. Back home, no one had any idea of the problems here, of all of the people vanishing in the woods or the danger. If they had, they would have asked someone else with more specialized experience to be deputy chief SO, who is now apparently the chief SO, who has to understand a planet full of who-knows-what. This job of mine," he paused, looking at his badge, "had originally just been intended as something to keep me busy."

"That is such bullshit, Ben," Janice answered with some anger. She didn't raise her voice often, but it was very noticeable she did –*IT CARRIED.*

"But it's still a better job than the one I left in North Dakota. I guess it's difficult to say this, but I've got to make things really work for myself here, because it's not going to happen any place else."

"Again, bullshit. You're just wrong." She quickly climbed out of bed and approached him, pushing hair off her face and fixing her very intense eyes onto his. Janice had no problem with up-close, face-to-face contact when irritated. "I think that the two years of sleep you had has clouded your memory, Officer Porterfield. I happen to know that you are very well thought of here, willing to go out of your way to help everyone out. You fixed primary electrical systems for the families in three houses before we'd even lived here for two weeks, because the only other expert in the town was swamped and couldn't get to them. These people really appreciate you for this, and I hear them talking about you with a sincere gratitude that is really touching. You've put up exterior walls, and even built that bridge that replaced the one over Orson River. Everyone knows that you're working constantly to keep them safe from whatever took down the last surveyors. I also think that you were very highly regarded back in the Grand Forks Police Department, even if people never really told you. You'd been badly wounded a long time ago, and still went back to that job. When you asked Levinson to leave early, he probably gave you a fantastic line to stick around, right?"

"Right," Ben answered. *REALLY, JANICE, YOU'RE TOTALLY WRONG!* "Well, I'm off to work, Jan. How do I look?" Janice looked him over appraisingly and smirked.

"Oh, like Old Ben, Wild and Woolly Wonder Nerd."

"You're so encouraging." They embraced and kissed.

"I'll see you tonight. Are you coming into town?" Janice shook her head.

"I'm studying pinnacles in this area, right around our house to be exact." Ben felt fear with that. *WHY DIDN'T WE MOVE INTO ONE OF THE VACANT HOUSES IN TOWN?* She could see his concern and said, "Don't worry. I'll be with two other Smithsonian people."

"Don't go too far off the trail or anywhere else by yourself, and bring something to protect yourselves." He kissed her again gently on the lips. "I love you."

Leaving the house, he felt a sharp ringing in his ears, a memory pushing itself to the surface. *TWENTY YEARS! IT WAS A NINETEEN YEAR RETIREMENT! 'GAVE YOU A FANTASTIC LINE TO STICK AROUND,' --TOTALLY WRONG!*

He entered his supervisor's office in Grand Forks, a neat and friendly environment with computer pictures, drawn by Lieutenant Levinson's two grandsons, so numerous as to make wallpaper. One boy in pottery class had made a lumpy, over-sized coffee mug for his grandfather, looking like it would leak out all of its contents before the owner could take the first drink. Levinson had been Ben's boss since first starting in SWAT. He had been recently promoted to district captain, increasing the span of his command by five times. It was effective in two months, and his old job would be filled by someone closer to Ben's age. Levinson was always courteous to him, very professional, and very impersonal. He gave a microscopic smile after allowing Ben in.

"Hello, Officer Porterfield, how's life on the plains?" Ben had conducted most of his investigations by the trains, surrounded by lots of farm country, always after the fight, but never in it - **EXCEPT ONCE**. He briefly explained how his wife had been given an opportunity by the Smithsonian to study botany on that very distant planet, Anteros. He had been with the police for eighteen years and would be for nineteen years before the flight was to depart from Earth, and asked if it were possible to work out a nineteen year all-at-once retirement package.

"Tell you what," Bruce had said with that affected smile, "Let's make it an even twenty. You've given this department good work and I think you've earned it. This is our gift to you: a bonus year." And that was that. No struggle to keep him around at all, in fact, an incentive for him to leave! Ben was not sure what his reaction would have been if he had been offered two of those horrible bonus years instead of one, in exchange for leaving right then and there, but he knew it wouldn't have been very polite.

Ben breathed in the morning fragrance of Anteros as he walked into the garage. His head was still buzzing with memories as he threw his leg over the seat and flipped on the power. The light bike vibrated slightly, and then lifted him a foot above the floor. It made a steady hissing from underneath, the air shooting up loose dirt as though it were subjecting it to a water hose. The curved bottom side was lined with nozzles and vents, spewing out enough air to lift their combined weight off the ground. His feet rested on two stubby wings, with powerful air jets underneath to provide lateral stability. The light bike had no wheels. It was the ultimate all-terrain vehicle, one that never touched the ground. But it took getting used to, since no tires meant no friction. Accidentally drifting off the trail and sailing all over the fields and hillsides was too easy. These bikes had been outlawed on all major roads and highways back on Earth, but the Mother Nature of Anteros, with all her thick jungles, prosecuted nearly everything but the light bike here.

He drove up to the trail and carefully looked for on-coming cycles. As safety officer, he had posted a speed limit of thirty MPH. It was sadistically slow and most people ignored it, rocketing by at way over sixty, but Ben wasn't in a good enough position in town to start handing out speeding tickets. He rolled the bike over to the right and squeezed the right handle, which decreased the thrust under the wing and caused him to tilt a bit. On the path he let up on the bar and held onto the outside handle grips. He pushed in gently with his left thumb on the accelerator button and the whine of air jets in back catapulted him forward. The air rushing past his ankles into the intake actually made him chilly. The bike was supposed to compensate for dents and bumps in the terrain below by increasing or decreasing the thrust to the appropriate jets, but Ben found out the hard way that this reaction wasn't instantaneous. At thirty MPH the front end dropped down, and then the jets overcompensated, sending the nose sailing back up into the air. It was like riding a wild horse. He was losing stability fast and released the accelerator. The bike drifted forward at a forty-five degree angle to the road, so he pushed the right button, sending a strong retro rocketing pulse of air out from the front. He glided backwards, half-off the trail before gently bumping against a thin sweetnut tree.

"A lot of getting used to, but that's okay, I have the rest of my life here to practice." He launched himself again, making it almost to town before he had to stop.

Ben had never cared for the Assistant Safety Officer, Scott Kubick. This thirty-two-year-old was not a very enthusiastic person, Ben noted when Scott reported for duty two months ago. Not friendly at all. He almost had to apply the thumb screws just to find out that he had been some ace with the New Orleans Police Department. He was an avid runner, and complained about being able to only do lap after lap around town or the landing area because nothing else was cleared of the flora. He was quite gifted in the workings of machines, but very but was extremely aloof and didn't readily offer his services. Scott had met his now-fiancée while preparing on the transport before they had even left orbit from Earth. Linda was the opposite of her future groom: a warm and brilliantly conversational woman who had been recruited by NAS reconnaissance because she was an entrepreneur, a former city council member of Anchorage, Alaska, and knew a lot about town economics to keep things moving along. Scott was so difficult, Ben couldn't understand how these two could get along. *OPPOSITES SOMETIMES*

ATTRACT, Ben would muse, *BUT THEY USUALLY DRIVE EACH OTHER CRAZY BEFORE TOO LONG*. Ben walked into the two-room town safety office and saw Scott sitting behind a wooden desk on the far side of the room. He had an image recorder mounted in the center of the desktop and it projected a three-dimensional picture of an enormous rat in perfect color and size. This monstrous rodent hovered motionlessly two feet above the chipped wooden surface and was perhaps four feet long, not including the tail. It had two visible mouths and four eyes. Lupus Rodentia - the wolf rat.

"Hey," he quietly acknowledged. Ben walked toward him, transfixed on the picture of this ugly native of Anteros. It resembled an earth rat in general shape, but this gnawer was twenty times larger! It was coated not with fur but a thin blanket of cilia, making its pasty white skin very creepy. The stooped nose and two-inch-long incisors gave it a ferocious look. The air-breathing undermouth was visible, revealing the tube leading down into its four lungs.

"Cute," Ben said. "Just like the mice back home."

"Watch this," Scott said, tapping a switch on the recorder with his foot. The holograph changed, showing the rat poised on its hind legs. Its forward eyes were large and hostile and its upper mouth was wide open, exposing two upper and two lower canines. It was angry about something. What was more disturbing about this creature was its tail, long

70

and thin and bald, which looked exactly like an earth rat's, except this one was as thick as Ben's arm and another four feet long! Ben stood up straight. "We need to get more scanners out there covering the woods to find either Will or his remains, and then I'm going to interview Jamie and their neighbors again." Scott looked frustrated.

"I'm here at four-thirty every morning and I placed the last batch of the scanners at five, so we know everything that happens here on the ground for a radius of a mile. You've already talked with Jamie and her next-doors twice, she doesn't have anything else to say and wants to be left alone, and made that clear to me the last time when I tried. I want to solve this as much as you do, but I'll take five minutes when I need to so's to relax the brain."

"No problem. Anything else?"

"Anything else what?"

"Has anything come up after I left yesterday?"

Scott shrugged. "No." Ben turned and walked to his desk and pulled out a hand-written list of tasks. He was going to continue his investigation into the disappearances of most of the colonists from the Second Survey.

At least there was no crime on Anteros caused by humans. People selected as surveyors did not include career criminals, terrorists, or sociopaths. No murders, assaults, burglary, or shoplifting. Ben wondered what would happen if he ever needed to arrest someone, since there was no jail at all. He'd probably have to lock the perpetrator in his garage for a week or two. As if he wasn't going to be busy enough, he also had to examine the materials to be used in the construction of the first large-scale electronuclear power plant twenty miles away, due to be completed in around twelve years.

His phone went off, an old-fashioned BEEP! BEEP! BEEP!" He looked down its display for the origin: Argo, the same area as the future power station. He set it flat on the table, which automatically answered it and placed it in speaker mode. It's difficult, he thought, not having a thick blanket of satellites circling Anteros. All of the orbiters that the *Agenor* had placed, like those of its predecessor, were almost burned out immediately because of the extreme solar activity, or rendered useless because of the very widely fluctuating magnetic fields caused by the planet, its iron-filled moon, and the asteroid field. Without these com and GPS transmitters, it was like living in the early nineteen-hundreds. At least the people from the second survey had put up four signal towers, so they still had telephones and basic signal detection.

"Argo supply office, Brenda Lathrop speaking," Argo, Ben thought. A small settlement with twelve or fifteen people living in it.

"Treefall safety office, SO Porterfield and SOA Kubick here. How can we help you?"

"Hello! Are you guys available to help us out?"

"Yes. What's up?"

"Some real problems. There are two people who are very sick and a third one is missing. Our casualties need to be moved to Treefall, but I'd like for a physician to come out here and diagnose their conditions before we move them. They're in bad shape." *MORE PEOPLE GONE,* Ben thought.

"Who's missing?"

"A landscaper, Hudson Manley, who lives here with his wife, Laura. She just came in a few minutes ago and told me that he was gone just after dawn. Hudson had gone to set up his equipment about a hundred yards or so in a clearing on the other side of some brush, and never came back for breakfast. We've searched the area up and down and couldn't find him. His bike is still here and his stuff is up and running, but he isn't there."

"Emergency locator?"

"Not working." *THIS IS WEIRD,* Ben thought. Emergency transmitter signals were subcutaneous and very difficult to muffle if inside a ten mile radius.

"Footprints?"

"Too many, mostly from us."

"These people who are sick, what are their symptoms?" Ben typed down a dozen different ailments, some of them, like severe bleeding from underneath the fingernails, sounded pretty nasty and alien, and forwarded them to Morahan.

"I'll be down there myself in an hour, and I'll bring a doctor with me. Get the folks ready to be moved to Treefall. Bye." He disconnected and looked at Scott, who now sat upright and looked at him with some intensity.

"You'd better stay here, I need to start an investigation and go over everything I know, talk to people, all of it." Ben said. The expression on Scott's face didn't change.

"If I go with you I could look over their electro nuke stuff. Two birds with one stone, right?"

73

Ben shrugged. "Maybe, but Argo is a pretty far away and I want one of us relatively close to Treefall. If there was a fire in town and we were both away, who would put it out?"

"Maybe some of these colonist whiz-kids could do it. They're smart and it's not like we have the only fire extinguisher in town."

Ben shook his head. "I'd really prefer to have one of us around. If you want, you can go to Argo and I'll stay here." It was a big mistake even suggesting that. He had handled cases of disappearances many times before when he had been loaned out to that area in the Grand Forks Police Department. He knew what questions to ask, and how to deal with bereaved, sometimes irrational loved ones. He knew what clues and signs to look for. His experience in such matters had formed a grim, unprinted resume, and he hoped that his credits in the subject of missing persons were transferrable to the University of Anteros. Scott finally gave in with a shrug.

"You're the one with about twenty years' work experience." *ABOUT TWENTY YEARS!* Ben felt a surge of dislike for this kid. "You make the call." Ben phoned the infirmary and ran down the list of symptoms with the chief of surgery, Doctor Morahan. The head physician said he would send his only assistant M.D. to the safety office. Ben stood and looked at him.

"I'll be back in five or six hours. Give me a call if anything hot comes up."

"Like a raging inferno consuming the town?" Kubick replied with zero trace of humor.

"Exactly." There was a hard knock on the door. Ben opened it to reveal the always cheerful face of Doctor Ervin.

Dean Ervin extended his hand. *I MUST HAVE SHAKEN THAT SKINNY HAND FIVE HUNDRED TIMES BY NOW,* Ben thought, shaking it again. *BUT HE REALLY DOES SEEM LIKE A PRETTY GOOD GUY.* Dean stood on the porch, and Ben briefly compared his spindly, wiry physique to one of the thin wooden beams holding up the roof behind him.

"Come on in, I'm just getting a few things together. You seem kind of eager this morning."

"Well, I was up all night cloning, so I have to bounce off the walls just to keep from falling asleep," Dean answered. Ben pointed toward the back desk.

"Doctor Ervin, this is Scott Kubick, Assistant Safety Officer." Dean flashed his big grin and energetically stomped across the long room with his hand held out. Scott gave him a tired look and forced himself to return the gesture. Ben loved it. No words were exchanged.

"Cloning what?" Ben asked. Dean swung around and marched back to him.

"I'm in the middle of rebuilding a new hand for Kevin Parkin, know him? No? Well, he's a hydrologist who was surveying the water table higher up. Anyhow, he forgot to use wasp repellent yesterday evening and got himself zapped by one of the charming natives. An ivory wasp must have hit him with its full sac of acid. By the way, did you spray this morning?" Ben nodded. "Good. I always

75

bring a canister with me in case I run into someone who didn't. People tend to be a little put off when I just walk up and spray them without their permission, but I don't care, it's just too dangerous. Back to Kevin, he had most of his hand dissolved - all of the skin and muscle and even the bone were melted completely away- really mangled. What made my job even more difficult was that I had him doped up so high on pain killers, he was like two-hundred pounds of Jell-O. I locked what was left of it in the cloner and then laid out the architecture of what his new hand would look like on a computer model. Are you familiar with the process?"

"Intimately. I had some cloning work done myself several years ago."

"Is that right? Have you --"

"We can talk about that later," Ben interrupted, "so does your story have a happy ending?"

Dean nodded. "Replacing an entire actual living limb, the nightmare scenario in clinical cloning, takes days, sometimes weeks. Today we got the bone structure grown, and then contained. I had to sit next to him and watch the display for six hours to make sure the cells grew and fused correctly. I'll let everything set for a few days –like letting plaster dry- and then we'll work on rebuilding the nerves, musculature and then the skin. Contrary to popular belief, the cloning process cannot be performed by a well-trained monkey, because appendage replacement involving bone and marrow gets really complicated. Once, back in Richmond, I replaced a man's entire leg all the way up to a hip that had been crushed and severed in a construction accident.

It took a month of excruciating bone and tissue regeneration, and it still wasn't perfect. His new leg was a millimeter longer than his right after the paint had dried, and that might not sound like much, but believe me, you notice something like that. He did." Ben looked at Dean's two small pouches.

"You're not bringing very much out there."

"I'm bringing a full spectrum of anti-bios and pain-killers, nitrogen treatment array, a basic first aid kit, and some extra supplies for both. It's not like I'm a traveling medicine show. I can't cure them with whatever I have on me and send them on their merry way. They're going to have to come back with us to the hospital so we can find out exactly what the problem is. From what you described it could be anything from influenza to endo-parasites roosting in the bowels. One ambulance is off picking up Jessica Newton, who from what it sounds like broke her leg, and the other one is being repaired, so one of these people will have to ride with me. Either you can bring the other, or I can recruit someone there to do it."

"It'll have to be someone else, Dean. Unfortunately someone else has gone missing and we have to start another investigation."

"Another one? Our time here has gotten very hard pretty fast. I can see why being a safety officer takes so much time." They both started walking toward the door and Ben gave Scott a last glance.

"Five or six hours. See ya'." Scott casually heaved up his right arm to form a sarcastic salute. Ben felt the resentment again.

Their destination took them down a trail that Ben had never been on before. Dean led the way on his very brightly painted white cycle. It was a real attention-grabber, a "PLEASE EAT ME" shade of white as Ben had remarked just before they took off. But Dean knew how to ride, probably being one of those maniacal bikers who had buzzed by Ben's house at three times the speed limit, and was now flying down the dark path at seventy miles an hour. Trees and plants whizzed by at an alarming speed, and the trail was so narrow, that Ben could almost feel them brushing against his arms. *ONE SLIP,* he thought, *AND THEY'LL BE PULLING ME OUT OF A KNOTHOLE ON A PINNACLE.* At slower speeds, Ben's bike engine made a gentle, almost quiet sound, but now it really roared with a hurricane of air being thrown out of the pipe. Doctor Ervin was a hundred yards ahead of him, but the gaseous tidal wave spewing out from his exhaust pounded Ben's windshield.

They sped into a hilly region. Savanna turned into mountains, but the foliage remained thick and dark. After several more miles Dean slowed suddenly. Ben braked hard and almost lost control to avoid rear-ending him. The path opened up into a small clearing that contained a dozen large wooden buildings. Ben came to a stop and let his bike drop to the ground. He looked toward the outskirts of Argo and saw people pushing through the thick brush. They were maybe seventy yards apart, fanning outward from this tiny village. He wanted to take a minute or two to chew out Dean for that insane driving, but instead walked toward these men and women.

"Your patients are probably in one of those dwellings, so why don't you check them out while I find out who the boss is." Ben approached a gentleman in very worn-looking gray coveralls, who looked to be in his middle seventies, pretty stocky, and hair that was mostly white. He had a very determined look emerging from a wall of blue plants and turned, about ready to move back in.

"Hello!" Ben called. The man turned to him. "I'm Safety Officer Ben Porterfield, here in response to your sick call and the disappearance." The man's expression didn't change.

"I'm Nathan Tunnell, one of the geologists up here. Yeah, Manley turned up missing, so we'll be out here looking until we find him. I should say that I'm looking for his remains, since no one who's gone too long ever comes home." He turned and headed back in between two blue-moss covered shrubs. Ben followed.

"Well you're the guy I'm looking for, since I know that you are the senior person here, and I'll help out. I have a favor to ask, though." Nathan didn't respond. "I see people moving around all over the place making a lot of noise. Are you armed?" Tunnell turned and placed his hand on a holster slung down from his belt. Ben looked at the black polymer grip, its glossiness and checkering, and felt a sudden spark. He only needed to look at the angle of it, and brightened. "An old-time, Wesson compensated four'n'a quarter, on the heavy F1 frame. They only made those with the ten inch barrel."

"That's not bad, Officer Porterfield," Tunnell answered.

"My dad had one."

"A sturdy four-and-a-quarter will put the stop on any local looking for a snack," He resumed his march, fixing his eyes straight ahead, "And I go by Nate."

"I'm Ben. Is everyone else armed?"

"Yes."

"It's dangerous to be out here by yourselves. Do me a favor and pair up." The man turned, aiming his large dark eyeballs into Ben's.

"Pair up? That won't do at all. If we spread out we'll increase our rate of coverage and find Hud that much quicker. No, things are fine the way they are."

"Until you start shooting each other."

"We're not a bunch of goddamned idiots out here, SO. We know the difference between a human and a wolf rat." He walked at a much faster pace, almost as if trying to lose Ben.

"If you move in groups you'll also be able to cover each other's backsides." No answer. Nate had made his decision, and that's how it was going to be.

Nate Tunnell had been one of the earlier colonists who, unlike many of those people, didn't jump onto the *Agenor* when it returned to civilization. He wore a thick, tattered jump suit with the sleeves down. His hair was plastered down with a heavy layer of insect and animal repellent to prevent some wasp from scalping him. His face was drenched in sweat.

"I surveyed your town," he said as they walked back to the buildings. "Treefall, isn't it? A lot of my friends built that place five or six years ago, several hundred of us. We have several big warehouses, mostly empty now, but used to be filled with all of the buildings that are now sitting in and around your vicinity. We were putting up houses and structures EVERYWHERE. Didn't seem like anything could stop us, but later we learned some things about living on Anteros. We were the Second Survey."

Ben was in the presence of a legend. The second group landed several years after the loss of the First Survey and positioned themselves near what was to be Treefall. The Argo group had been composed of geologists, carpenters and artisans. They built the large platforms to accommodate the landers from interstellar transports, one near Treefall and one near Argo. But the Second Anteran Survey had suffered a lot of losses when first immersed here, with many perishing from nickel poisoning in the beginning. Most of them just disappeared, Nathan told him, gone without a trace.

"There are maybe twenty of us original folks left, at least in Argo, and thirty-nine more stayed in Treefall. It's funny, but it's actually been about nine years since I've received a pay statement, but that doesn't mean anything here. When Astro Space sent us here, they didn't think about things like economics, so we pretty much had to do everything on a barter system."

81

"We have a financial system in place. We get paid, now, provide services, and compete –pretty much a capital-based country like back home. I'll see that you all are reimbursed for any lost pay."

"Either way, I don't care. We in Argo survive here in our own way."

"That's another reason why I came, how are you set for supplies? I've tried contacting for six weeks but never got an answer. You've been here for so long, do you need medicine, or any food bars? You can come into town whenever you want and procure what you need for free, so why don't you?"

"When we left our ship we were given enough basic medicine to last for our entire lifetimes. As for food, well, the food bar concept hadn't even been approved by the FDA when we left, so were just given standard provisions for ten years, which ran out after half that. Since then, we've gone native. We're dining in."

"You've been eating things from Anteros? I mean, these plants and animals are nickel. How do you, well, keep from dying horribly?"

"Do you take Cyroxin 213?"

"Yes, but that's just because of the nickel in the atmosphere and the ground and the stuff that brushes against you."

"You take it once a month for that. We have a Cyroxin synthesizer, so we can make as much of it as we need, because we learned that if digested once a day you can eat whatever you want here and the metals will just purge right out of your system, not because we wanted to, but because we had to.

Mostly plants, and sometimes small animals. Keep your food bars, officer, we just don't need them." Ben thought for a moment.

"What does it taste like?"

"After hamburgers and spaghetti heavy on meatballs –my personal favorites fifteen years ago- food here doesn't even compare, and I don't mean that in a good way. It is very strange in every regard, and took me a full year to get used to. Trust me when say that when you try a spiral snake for the first time, it will be the weirdest and most difficult taste you'll have ever had," Nate warned. Ben smiled slightly out of his right and answered,

"Trust me, you haven't had my wife's fish casserole."

Nathan and Laura Manley walked with Ben along the route Hudson had taken. Laura was quite calm, and stated that she was quite certain her husband was gone for good. All of the people who were there earlier had tracked up the place and it was impossible to tell one print from the next. They went to the clearing where Hudson had been working. The automated transit system that he'd brought with him was set up perfectly on its tripod and had been activated.

"Have you heard any strange noises? I mean more unusual than normal?" Ben asked.

"The only thing we hear at night are the rats," Nate answered. "Christ, every night for a decade, the only sounds are the grinding noises of those big monsters sharpening those tusks of theirs. But they haven't been making such a racket lately."

"Yeah?"

"Sometimes they all just bug out and go into hiding. It's like that everywhere on the planet, I think. One day they're here playing their teeth like a fiddle, and the next they're just gone. Maybe they're laying low and watching us, I don't know."

"You two are pretty familiar with wolf rats. Well, from what I've seen of them a person might be able to fight off one of them, but what if they moved against you in a group, like a pack of wolves?" Ben asked. Laura and Nate exchanged a quick glance.

"Rats hate each other and are ferociously independent. One's company, two's a crowd with that species," Laura answered.

"She's right," Nate said. "I've never seen more than one at a time. They're partial to carrion and usually hover over a dead bird or animal. A rat won't attack you unless you really get it aggravated."

"What about ivory wasps? Could they have swarmed him?" Laura asked.

"If that's the case we'd still find something of a body. They could douse him in acid, but they can't completely dissolve an entire human." Ben said."

"Whatever is out there, it got to his emergency locator transmitter. No way could he have walked ten or fifteen miles. If he were lost, standard operating procedure would be for Hudson to have just called us and then stay in place for the searchers to find him." Nate was right. This was odd.

And now they walked toward a honey willow tree, identical to the one close to Ben's house. Even the surrounding terrain looked the same, with all

84

other shrubs and trees courteously holding back fifty yards. It was almost as if the willow had a mind of its own, requiring a specific landscape and scenery. The only thing growing in its private glade was grass, with this drooping, dripping tree, majestically standing in the center. Ben could hear the humming of the honey wasps as they approached.

"He might have passed through here. I see footprints. Have any searchers been by?"

"I don't think so. This is about five hundred yards further from where we were," Nate answered. Ben stood silently. Cascading blankets of thin, lacy honey vines almost completely masked the trunk of the tree, but he could barely make out a silhouette of a tall and thin shaft of wood with no distinguishable color. Looking through this was like looking through a white linen sheet.

"You're more of a veteran to this environment than I am, Nate. I've studied a lot of books, but that doesn't replace experience. I know of wolf rats, harlequin lemurs, and those harrier bats, but have you ever seen anything larger?" Ben asked.

Nate stood silently for a moment. "Larger or more deadly? There are mites on Anteros that have some pretty lethal venom, but can't break human skin."

"Larger. The rat is around three or four feet long, and the harrier is about the same. Okay, fine, on Earth we have wolves and large birds like condors. But there are also Kodiak bears, Twenty-foot-long Indo-Pacific crocodiles and even dinosaurs long ago. Do you know what I'm saying?

There are things a lot bigger than just wolves and birds on Earth, and I think that there may be animals on Anteros that are much bigger than anything we've seen yet. I've looked at some of the houses of people who'd vanished years ago, and saw, I think, some gigantic claws marks on walls. Dozens of your people have turned up missing over the last ten years, and maybe they did see something larger, and it killed them or carried them off before they could report it."

"There is something else very big here," Nate said, "but I've never seen anything larger than the rats. After years of living on the surface, there is something roaming around that I just never saw, but I think that some people have, the ones who are never seen again." Ben turned back toward the willow.

"We have to be sure that we've searched everywhere." Nate's face grew very tense and his tired-wrinkled eyes widened with youthful alarm.

"You are insane," he said without his rustic accent. "Officer Porterfield, these are the most beautiful trees in the universe. The branches hang over like inverted seaweed, with this honey hanging down like a frozen waterfall, but don't be fooled; inside there is pure death. They didn't evolve to be pretty or to give nectar to the animals. They're symbiotic with the thousands of predators dwelling in there. Those sweets are there to lure an animal inside where it is promptly bushwhacked by those demons. I've heard it happen many times and I know those bastards are very indiscriminating as to what they tear apart. Send in robots."

86

"They get eaten almost immediately, we've tried."

"So will you."

"I wasn't going in there unprotected."

They walked for half a mile up a lightly graded hill before coming onto another plateau, whose surface had been artificially ground down to a very unnatural flat. It wasn't earthen-brown, either, it glowed silver against the two suns, reflecting their images like a highly polished mirror. This was another landing platform for Astro Space vehicles, a thousand feet on each side.

"You know, I helped build this place. Nine years ago, from out of the blue, four Space Recon ships come dropping down from the sky, without even bothering to phone us to let us know they were comin'. Surprised the crap out of us. This was before our people began disappearing, so we didn't have anything to warn them about." At each corner of the square was a two-story shed made entirely of smooth polytitanium composite. The two men walked toward one of them. "We built these store houses, working our butts off. But then, after we finished, you know what these ASR guys did? They filled them up with all kinds of goodies, locked them up, and didn't leave us a key!"

"I've got the key, the only one as far as I know," Ben answered. He knew what kind of a reaction this would get. He could almost hear the blood rushing up into Nate's face.

"Why in the name of hell did they give *you* the only blasted key, Porterfield?" Nate, Ben thought, probably figured that these sheds were filled with sumptuous cuisines, plush, comfortable beds and other aristocratic delights, that the big-shots felt were far too high-quality to be enjoyed by the likes of him and his ordinary entourage. He needed enlighten this irritated geologist, or risk having some kind of social revolution in the making.

"They would have left two, one with you as head of the Second, and other with the safety officer, Kevin Hedrick. If they didn't, then they made a mistake. But there's nothing in here you can use. All surface installations like this one for Astro-spacecraft have to store emergency equipment. Doubly so this far out from Earth."

"Why?"

"For the transport ship. There could be a bad accident in space that would endanger the possibility of it ever returning. Out here on Anteros, they would have to wait for twenty months, when they would be overdue at the Proteus Astro Space Center. Word would get back to Earth four months after that, and an emergency dispatch ship would get here after two more years. That's a hell of a long time, so they basically crammed enough spare parts into these things to literally build a makeshift interstellar spacecraft." They approached the blinking lights of the lock and Ben pulled out his magnetic key.

"What's in there that will protect you inside that tree? Are you going to haul in some kind of cannon?"

"Well, when we were still in space and heard about all of the problems here, I asked the captain of the *Agenor* about some heavier armament that we could be equipped with, much more so than impact weapons, either stowed there or on the surface. Something like a two-man-operated gamma will kill anything organic, no matter how big, but he told me that there was nothing he had, since they were civilian ASR, and the military hadn't been out here yet, because there hasn't been a need for it. There is some heavy-duty safety equipment here, so I'll use an engine suit," Ben answered. Nate was confused.

"What's that?"

"Engine suits are basically big, thick pressure suits. In the guts of a spaceship's engine, an engineering technician wears one of these whenever he's working close to the nucleon fusion components. It's a little warm inside those things, even when they're idling. In fact, it's hot enough to instantly flash stainless steel into iron steam. But the tech wearing this suit, exposed to hundreds of thousands of degrees, doesn't even get as much as a tan."

"So you're going to put on one of these suits of armor and then walk into a hornet's nest. You think it'll keep those wasps from getting to you?"

"Engine suits are incredibly tough. Put one on and you could probably take a walk on the surface of the sun. They're made of a hundred different complex metallic composites, and cost more than what I'll see in my lifetime."

"Just one thing, Porterfield, won't those federal ASR people mind you're using some of their pricey stuff for something like this?"

"Colonists get first priority by law. I've got to see first-hand what is going on inside that tree, and

89

determine if it's a threat to the general populace. Who knows, maybe whatever is preying on all of our people is in there. Besides, there are other suits in there, so it's not like I'll be risking the only one. By the way, I'll need help carrying it." This surprised Tunnell.

"How much do the damn things weigh?" An ordinary pressure suit could be lifted with one hand.

"A lot more than I do," Ben answered.

"Christ Almighty.

They had to drag it out of the building, since it weighed four-hundred pounds and was stiff enough to stand upright on its own. It was twice as wide as Ben, looking like something that he might have used for deep-sea diving. The metal was extremely reflective, probably for deflecting the ultra-energetic radiation in a fusion contact chamber. Once they were outside, Ben powered it up, and working a remote control, was able to start walking it on its own to the to the tree, which would take a while. An engine suit was super-strong, but very, very slow even at maximum speed, which was three miles an hour. He heard the whines of light bike engines and their elevation was high enough to afford Ben a view of the tops of the buildings in Argo and the path leading up to them. *HAD I KNOW THE ROAD WAS THIS MEANDERING,* Ben thought, *I NEVER WOULD HAVE TAKEN IT FASTER THAN TWENTY.* There were two light bikes, each holding a driver with a passenger seated to the rear.

"That'd be your doctor friend and Brenda helping him. I'd be guessing they're headed for

Treefall with the Dreiths. I was kind of hoping he'd be able to give them what they need up here. It's just lost manpower, that's all." Ben recalled what Dean had said earlier: "It's not like I'm a traveling medicine show."

"He knows what he's doing." He knew that Doctor Ervin hadn't slept because he was giving a man his hand back, and just when the Doc had probably thought of dropping off to Dreamland, he got this emergency call. *TOUGHER THAN HE LOOKS*. In fact, he'd never seen Dean act in a selfish or inconsiderate way toward anyone, and bent over backwards to help out people who needed it. *JANICE WAS RIGHT ABOUT HIM*. The bikes slowly made their way around the contours of the path.

"Your friend flies a bike kinda' conservatively, doesn't he?" Nate asked. Ben chortled loudly but said nothing. *OH, IF HE ONLY HAD SEEN OUR APPROACH!*

Standing before the honey willow gave him second thoughts about this whole idea, as the vacant suit stood next to him. In the back was a long, narrow hatch, awaiting Ben's entrance.

"One thing, officer, do you know how to even operate this thing?"

"Believe it or not, I took a day-long course on this a week before we entered orbit around this place. I learned how to work the finger controls pretty well from inside, and they are what actually control the movement. The executive officer of the ship had told me it was mandatory training, although at the time I didn't know why. I guess they wanted me prepped for a lot of possibilities, like walking my own dumb ass into a bee-infested tree." Ben slipped his left leg into the opening in the back, the sides deflecting slightly, hinting that the suit still had some qualities of fabric. Nate stood behind him, preparing to close it up.

"Anything else you want to say? The com system in this thing still needs a lot of programming to get it online, so once you're in there, you're alone."

"Give me fifteen minutes."

"And then what, say a quiet prayer?"

"Make it a loud one. Don't worry, in here I could do the back stroke in a pool of phosphoric acid. I doubt if the paint will even be scratched, but if I'm in there for too long, well, call SO Kubick in Treefall and figure out a way to get me out."

"Good luck." Ben stood up inside of his enclosure and the hissing of the air lock in back sounded. He was truly isolated.

First, he activated the video camera. He was probably going to be the first to actually see what was going on in the center of one of these bizarre trees, and had a feeling many people would be interested in what was really in there. His helmet camera gave him half a dozen readings located on the lower right field of his visor. There were other options available, like graphs of external suit stress and temperature, but he kept those turned off. There was also a passive electric air filter, located just under his chin. Carbon dioxide he exhaled passed through it, where the carbon atom was ripped from the two oxygens via an electric field, thus replenishing his air, and then was stored as graphite. It was nice to not have to carry an external oxygen supply. Electronic sensors lining the interior of the suit responded to his movements by triggering the correct motor. He stepped forward. The first strands of sweet vines wrapped around his helmet, blurring his view a bit. His pace was steady and he advanced into the tree. He was ten feet into the cloak of branches and vines but didn't notice anything peculiar. No huge insects swooped down at him. He moved in another five feet and the trunk of the tree became sharper. It stood fifty feet ahead, but was moving, swaying back and forth, shimmering behind the ultra-thin strings. He didn't like this, but stepped forward.

His eyes were fixed upon the wooden cylinder, and he wasn't looking at the ground. He felt a definite tapping sensation, though, starting down by his feet and randomly moving up his back. It was so light he didn't even give it a second thought, but then saw something at the very top of his visor. It was black and was very alive. A stick-like object with the diameter of his index finger waved in front of him. And then this creature moved and he saw the rest of it. It was a spider, with a circular body larger than a soft ball, and a leg span making it as big as an Alaskan king crab! The suit was so big and heavy that the spider had no perceptible weight, but it blocked out most of his field of vision. This gigantic bug had a twitching head covered with large, black eyes, and four penny-sized ducts on its stomach for breathing. What looked like four inch-long antennae poked out of the top of its head. It crawled diagonally down his chest and disappeared. But then the tapping increased. Every "tick-tick-tick" were footfalls. He made the mistake of looking down, but couldn't see his own legs. They were vibrating with seventy spiders clinging to him. They were trying to bite him, but weren't hurting him. His first instinct was to swipe them away, but his mechanized arms and legs weren't fast enough. Another spider covered his sight for a moment, and then jumped away. Ben was suddenly struck by a nightmarish image of walking into this environment with no suit at all. These magnificent and innocent-looking trees contained the most gruesome death anyone ever dreamed of. Another thought jumped into his mind: what if Nate hadn't sealed the engine suit properly, and a spider got in there with him! When he came within a dozen paces of the tree trunk the spiders left him and fearfully retreated. Nature's wild animals never flee like this without a really good reason, he figured. He took a close look at the trunk: it was vibrating because it was covered, one hundred percent, by a blanket of honey wasps. His entire suit hummed with their droning songs. All of the vines were behind him and he was staring at an unobstructed pillar of ten or twenty thousand fist-sized insects. They were angry. One second they were ten feet away, and the next they were all over him. They swarmed Ben and covered him from head to toe, stinging and biting. Now he felt a force of thousands of these wasps almost toppling him over backwards, the impact of each one pressing against his suit creating a loud CLACK! sound. This nerve-wracking noise repeated with such a frequency that it sounded like a hailstorm. He circled the trunk once, looking for anything that might have been a human skeleton, but there was nothing. The wasps pushed against his every move. They pressed at him so hard it was like walking against an eighty mile-an-hour wind.

"Time to leave. Oh yes, it is time to get the hell out of here." He turned around and started to walk as quickly as possible. After five more feet, the wasps were gone. They knew that they were now in enemy territory, the Land of the Spiders, and dashed for home. After covering two or three more steps, Ben lost his footing.

A force pulled him down on the left side, yet his leg remained fully extended. He had sunk into some kind of hole and his hip was now at ground level. Now the "tick-tick-tick" increased to ten times what it had ever been. His field of vision was blocked out completely and stayed that way. The spiders were back, this time with a vengeance. Army ants lived in colonies on Earth, as did these spiders on Anteros, and Ben had just pushed his leg into their home, a deep pit two feet in diameter. He could still pivot his foot around, so it hadn't struck the bottom. He pictured in his mind some kind of Queen Spider, as large as an octopus, sitting at the bottom of the nest, giving orders to her valiant soldiers to slay the shiny invader by whatever means necessary. Ben couldn't get up. The suit didn't give him the coordination to reach down and push himself out of the hole, so he was going to be staying there for a while. His only other option was to pop open the pressure door, spring out, and make a dash for safety outside of the tree -*NOW THAT'S AN INSANE IDEA! THESE SPIDERS WILL SWARM INTO THE SUIT THE SECOND I TRY. NO WAY. I'LL STAY IN HERE FOR DAYS AND DIE OF DEHYDRATION BEFORE IT COMES TO THAT!* After several long minutes he could feel a pressure pushing up on his foot, almost as if it had been plugging up a pipe filled with flowing water. *THESE LITTLE BASTARDS ARE TRYING SOMETHING NEW!* Ben thought. *MAYBE THEY'RE SMART ENOUGH TO FIGURE OUT A WAY TO CRACK ME OPEN LIKE A SOFT-BOILED EGG!* The force was from thousands of trapped arachnids who were determined to get out. They were strong! They were lifting Ben and the suit's combined weight out of the hole! After several more seconds he was completely out. He landed upright and tottered forward and backward several times, an experience that was almost as terrifying as being stuck: if he fell over backwards, he would be as helpless as a turtle in such a position, with his arms and legs flailing uselessly about. He stabilized himself and resumed his march toward the edge of the tree, despite a ferocious spider assault. Daylight! He cleared the last of the honey vines and was outside. Nate, standing twenty feet away, turned and fled. Ben looked down. The spiders that had been clinging to him were gone.

Nate spent half a minute looking the suit over from a distance before he would even approach. Then he popped open the back panel and spoke as a pale, trembling Benjamin Porterfield slowly climbed out. The outer skin of the suit was no

96

longer sparkling white, but black and slippery against his hands, splotched and splashed with dark fluids from the warriors of the arachnid army.

"I've never seen anything like that. You were covered in bugs! Completely! I couldn't even tell it was you when you first walked out. It took them a few seconds, but when they saw they were outside their place, they broke for home, scared as all hell it seems." Ben didn't answer -he was shaking too badly and couldn't breathe right. "What did you see?"

Ben shook his head. "I didn't find anything resembling a body, but who can tell? The insects and spiders inhabiting this tree are so voracious there wouldn't be anything left. You remember what the fire ants were like back on earth? How they made those little sandy hills along the sides of sidewalks? Those things live the same way, except their hole is large enough to drop a watermelon down."

"Lord," Nathan exclaimed. "And you think that Hudson could have wound up down there?" The idea of falling down the spider hole, all of him and not just a leg, was immensely terrifying to Ben and sent a ripple of nausea through him.

"I didn't see him, or any clothes or remains. Believe me, the spiders' assault is extreme. I would be strips of flesh by now if it weren't for this suit. But there were no remains at all of Hudson."

"Do you think they ate him?"

Ben shrugged. "I don't know, possibly. But we've each got these transponders, and the material they're made from is pretty strong. How could they chew one of those?"

"Maybe the wasps dissolved it. That's all I can think of."

"He never would have made it past the spiders. Even if he did, I think I would have found some parts of clothes." Ben looked at the tree and remembered the thousands of footsteps singing to him through his suit. "Still, if we don't find anything else, I'd say this tree is a real good suspect." They walked toward the nearly-black engine suit, preparing to walk it back. Ben's knees suddenly gave out and he doubled over, tasting a large ball of especially pungent vomit welling up in his throat. It was hard, but he gulped and held it down.

Chapter 5: Recollections

They entered Nathan's small office. Considering how long he's been on this planet, Ben thought, he has very basic furniture, just a hand-made desk and a chair, and then saw that the walls were covered with dozens of hand-drawn pictures of the landscape and animals, vivid and very detailed, with the shadows of the leaves casting down, and the perfect clarity of the perspective views of trees up close and those in the distance. This was real art, sketched by people who were struggling to live, that could probably fetch many millions back on Earth, but he knew that Nate would never part with them, nor would anyone else there. Ben respected that, as he and his own survey would probably create many such drawings themselves that would always to belong to them and this world.

Nathan plopped in a big wooden chair behind the desk.

"I've got a little souvenir for you to take back to Treefall. Maybe your doctor can make something of it." He reached into the bottom drawer and pulled out a large white ovoid object that glistened with white ivory. It was fifteen inches tall and had two eye sockets.

"Nice. What is it?"

"It's the skull of one of those talking monkeys, Ben. We found this in a real nasty fresh dung pile about a week ago. It was weird because the bugs and beetles wouldn't go near it. Take this back to Treefall and try to find out what killed this guy. You want to know if there is new creature out there, well, this might be another clue." Ben took the remains of the harlequin lemur. *THIS MIGHT BE THE EVIDENCE I'M LOOKING FOR.*

"I wish I could leave those store units out there unlocked for you for emergencies, but they close automatically, and only my key and fingerprint can open them again. For now I need to get some equipment from Treefall, like some thermal visors. I'll be back tomorrow and then we can really search this place for Hudson."

"Fair enough." Nathan stood up and rounded the desk, and for the first time today he extended a hand. "It was nice to meet you." Ben smiled and shook it.

Ben flew his bike twice as fast as usual and kept excellent control, having learned a lot just from observing Dean and his extreme driving. He looked at the trees and shrubs speeding by, but then the vegetation suddenly disappeared and was replaced by darkness. In another instant this void was replaced by the familiar blue vines and leaves. Ben released the accelerator and increased the pressure on the thumb button, causing the booster to push against him from the front, a beautifully controlled stop. He traveled in reverse for half a minute back to the emptiness, a doorway into the wilderness.

It was over thirty feet tall and almost as wide, nearly large enough for Ben to fit his house into. Branches and plants had been ripped out or mashed into the ground. This large entrance, or exit, was deep, too, leading to shadows underneath the adjacent trees. He could see in for maybe ten feet, but then the light was drowned out completely. He shut down the bike's power supply, and it dropped closer and closer to the ground. He stepped off and looked. *NO WAY WAS THIS DAMAGE HERE WHEN I CAME FROM TREEFALL.* He looked across the path to see if there was a similar tear on the other side, but saw nothing. Then he stepped into the opening and was surprised at how quickly the light faded. Just one pace inside and he could barely see his own feet, so he backed out, and then he saw the footprint.

There was a single, massive indentation. What this impression would have looked like on a sandy beach! The press mark had the diameter of a manhole cover and pushed into the ground seven or eight inches. Spreading radially outward from the imprint were eight two-inch--wide marks, each extending out another ten inches. Twelve feet further into the opening in the foliage, where the light ceased, was another such footprint. Ben probed his mind for any kind of animal in the universe with a foot this size and shape. Until now, the largest animal on Anteros known was a wolf rat, but its foot was scarcely larger than his hand. This one was much larger, and by the depth into which it had sunk, was very heavy. He listened to the surrounding sounds. There were the choruses of crickets and beetles, but no rasping -no wolf rats or rustling around him. He finally looked up, but was immersed in night and unable to see the light pushing through the trees above. He had unconsciously walked further into the opening and was staring down at the second footprint.

He meant to pull his Chamber's 4.25, but accidentally drew out the stun gun that was tightly clutched in his right hand. The blackness was gravely quiet. His only thought was to get out of there, but didn't want to turn his back and run - leaving a sea of wilderness behind him. Whatever belonged to this print could come up behind him and grab or bite or slash. He intended to step backwards, but as if pulled by an unseen force, stepped forward instead. It was darker. No sounds. He stepped moved again. The trees, large and small, were black shadowy fingers in the background. The temperature dropped. Something grabbed his ankle. He jerked down, and saw that what felt like long, hard claws was really a cluster of roots. He breathed deeply, feeling his heart calming. But he felt more than just relief, he was physically washed over by a comfortable feeling, a gentle warm breeze sweeping over him. Then it turned into a hot, wet wind blowing at him from behind, a sultry air onto his scalp and neck. Now he realized that he was being breathed on.

He swung around, facing the dimly illuminated hole -nothing. Now his back was against the unknown. What had been behind him had probably skulked behind him again. He imagined it very clearly: he turned again to face the darkness, and would see it -the unknown monster staring back at him from a few feet away. He twisted his knee and literally leaped back out on the trail, but what he now saw was all wrong: red! Everything was red! The path had once been brightened by purplish-white sunlight, but now it, the sky, the facade of trees and the ground were crimson. Even his bike had been changed. Behind him he heard movement. It was lumbering and slow, crushing everything just beyond the entrance. Ben jumped onto the saddle and powered up. He accelerated forward so fast that the bottom of the light bike hacked against the ground. *RED!*

The red light persisted and there was a moment when Ben figured that his fear and had finally pushed him to insanity. His speed verified this: he was going a hundred miles an hour. He sped into a wide open meadow and began to slow. *TIME TO STOP –LOSING IT COMPLETELY, SO TAKE IT COOL, THE FIRST STEP IS TO STOP.* As he glided to a halt he kept mumbling, "Breathing, breathing." He stopped and looked up at the sky. Orpheus was gone --the whole brilliant white star was missing, and only the red giant hung overhead, dim enough so that he was not blinded when looking straight at it, and then he smiled.

"Red night!" he yelled. The smaller Orpheus was hiding behind the small red giant, bathing the planet Anteros in a dim red light for two weeks. But what'd really thrown his mind into seeing red was pure panic. *WHEN WAS THE LAST TIME SOMETHING LIKE THIS HAPPENED? NINETEEN YEARS AGO!* It was a kind of sick fear people never experience, if lucky. He sat on the moist ground and leaned back against the bike, catching his breath and trying to slow his heart. He had dropped his stun gun back there, and now agonized over this. Then he felt it again, the hot tickling of his neck hairs beneath the wind, and he almost gave himself whiplash when he swung around, but only the bike was there. He still felt the strange sensation and it wouldn't go away. It was a physical manifestation that, he hoped, would not stay with him for the rest of his life.

MY REACTION BACK THERE WAS SHAMEFUL –DISGRACEFUL! PANICKY AND HELPLESS! He had stood in the darkness, felt that dampness, and the next feeling was the "Thump!" of his stun gun dropping onto his boot. His eyeballs were physically bulging out of his head and pushing over the lower lids. Over the years, he had prided himself on improving at anything that he did, but now realized that in important matters nothing had changed: he lacked courage. It was something people either had or hadn't, an endowment never given to him. Under calmer circumstances, self-discipline had enabled him to keep bad memories and feelings tightly contained, but now he was hurt and vulnerable. Very suddenly, Ben found himself trapped in a world of many years ago.

"Officer Benjamin Porterfield is our department genius," Lieutenant Levinson said. "When I saw his application I made sure he was sent right up here after he graduated from General Operations. It's department policy to recruit people with science and engineering degrees, and it really paid off with this gentleman." The twenty-three year-old Benjamin Porterfield turned away from the computer and stood, realizing that he was about to address the district captain.

"I wish I could think of something to refute everything the lieutenant's said about me, but nothing comes to mind." Both of the older men laughed.

"And then there's that self-deprecating humility," Levinson continued. "We'll have to work on that." Ben shook hands with one of the legends in the world of terrorism analysts, Captain Leonard Hall.

"Good to meet you, Benjamin. I'd heard about your development up here and figured I'd take a first-hand look. It's a real pity no one will ever see your work published."

Ben shrugged. "I'm sure I'd have a large audience of loyal fans," he answered.

"All of them bad boys," Levinson replied. Ben stood and his boss didn't fail to continue the praise. "Officer Porterfield is also a fair hand with firearms, one hell of a pistol marksman. That's why his status is as an active law enforcement officer, as opposed to just a hired nerd."

"I'm still a nerd at heart, Captain," Ben answered.

"Sounds like you have a splendid future here, officer. Let me verify this for the record: you are fully cleared for Special Weapons and Tactics?"

"Yes, sir."

"Let's see what you've got."

There was a conference room completely cleared of tables and chairs. It had four blank walls, a ceiling, and nothing else: the demo room. Ben and his colleagues entered and closed the door.

105

"Claustrophobic," Captain Hall said. Ben held up three pairs of darkly tinted glasses. "Don't worry, you'll be outside soon enough." He handed them out, and they slid the rails over their ears.

"I can't see a thing," Hall griped.

Ben spoke out, "Let's see the introduction." Somewhere in the room was a computer that heard this, because their visors suddenly lit up. They were now standing in a prairie, a grassy flatland stretching all the way to a distant horizon and merging with a cloudy blue sky. Ben looked over his shoulder and saw the two officers standing ten feet away.

"Nice, very nice. These are the best picture glasses I've ever seen," Hall said.

"Still feel claustrophobic?"

"As a matter of fact I feel a little chilly. This, scenery, about what time of the year did you program it for?"

"Early autumn. The temperature is a balmy fifty-five degrees with a ten mile an hour south-western breeze. Twenty percent chance of snow by the end of the week."

Levinson chortled. "You crack me up, another reason why we hired you." Tall grass and wheat wafted gently under a simulated wind that none of them could feel, but the animation was so real and the picture so clear, that it was impossible to believe there were still four walls confining them.

Ben started to walk and the others followed. There were pits and rocks in their path, but the floor of the conference room was still flat. The small rubble looked three dimensional, but it was still level with every step. They walked for several paces and stood on the edge of a lightly-graded hill, the top of which offered a splendid view of Grand Forks in the far distance. Much closer than that, though, was a large, glassy cylinder, half buried in earth, which stretched from the city and disappeared to the north. They could see a good ten miles of this birail housing in both directions.

"Now we get to the trains," Ben said. "The modern magnetic birail locomotive is housed in a circular case that is precisely ten meters in diameter. The only structural support uses two rails, at the inside top and bottom, which produce a magnetic field powerful enough to suspend the cars about two inches from each. A third acts on the rear, giving the train a continuous push, and a fourth slows it down." Ben looked up at the sky. "Birail, please." The cylinder suddenly lit up with a pulse of sunlight reflecting off a moving birail train, zipping along too fast for them to lock onto with their eyes. "They're pretty fast. The linear magnetic fields can kick those trains up to three thousand miles an hour if they're in a real big hurry. The normal cruising speed is around fifteen hundred to two-thousand, but I could be in Miami in forty-five minutes if I buy the right ticket."

"Faster than commuter planes," Hall remarked.

Ben nodded. "And more efficient. Divide the pressure we're feeling right now by a hundred, and you'll have what is in there. The losses from air friction are almost non-existent. Most of the energy goes into starting and stopping. For the next demo I'll have a train going fifty times slower. My specialty is figuring out terrorist attacks on them beforehand, not ex post facto."

Hall shook his head. "Terrorists. Birails aren't going to continue to be viable because they're so vulnerable. Look! Shooting at an exposed housing poking out of the ground like that is about as easy as shooting your big toe. Why in the hell don't the feds stick them completely under?"

"Maintenance, mostly. Some aesthetics, I guess. People love to watch the lakes and mountains zooming by," Ben answered, looking up. "Give me a slow train." Again they saw a train leaving the city, but this one was crawling. It was also the shape of a cylinder, but was indented in at the top and bottom to accommodate the rails. "Small weapons aren't a problem. The housing is stout and heavily built, and not even an anti-satellite particle device can cut through it." The train slowly moved toward their central line of sight. "The latest M.O. is to attach ultra-high energy shaped charges to the top of the supports." Ben paused. There was a small flash of light about a half mile in front of the locomotive. "Right there -detonation. Most of the blast is directed inward, effectively disrupting the housing and twisting apart the top rail." He paused again. The train made contact. The entire housing, for two miles, suddenly began to wrinkle. It looked like paper sliding on a table top, being pushed into a wall. The area around the train was flaring white with heat. "With no upper magnetics, the train is forced up into the newly-generated crevice before the lower rail can cut its field." The tube for thousands of feet was ripped out of the ground.

There was no more vehicle, only a glowing white mass that was now outside of its containment and moving forward. Brilliant strings of white fire raced ahead.

"Timing is critical," Ben said, his voice now dead serious. "Fatalities are always one-hundred percent. The wreckage has been spread out for twenty miles in some cases, like that place west of Kansas City last year. But if the attackers are more than a tenth of a second off, the train can stop in time and be saved. Still, birail terrorism successfully hits four locos a year, which translates to several thousand deaths."

"Okay, tell me about your project, Ben," Hall said. Ben looked up.

"Up close." They were instantly moved a thousand yards closer to the cylinder, which was once again intact. The image had been shifted so fast that Ben became dizzy. They were five feet from it, looking up at its huge curvature. There were thick titanomer support ribs spaced every twenty yards. Normally a person could see completely through an empty transparent birail housing to the other side, but not in his simulation! It shimmered with streaks of white light.

"I came up with a chemical coating that is deposited underneath the topmost layer of the structure, through which a very slight electrical current is applied. It is exaggerated here in the form of these wavy lines of light."

"Which does?" Hall asked.

"It detects stress in the material, stresses so slight that someone walking right next to it will activate it. It filters out only local distortions, so that wind shear doesn't send it cockeyed. That's it. The only people who are authorized to stand within two-hundred yards of birail track are maintenance workers, and their locations are sent to the city. Anything else is fed back to our computers, and a team is dispatched to check it out. A shaped charge will just bounce off the surface unless it is attached, and physical contact really drives the electrical signal nuts."

"What about false alarms? Kids too close and such?"

"We get them pretty often and it runs us into the ground checking every one out. Usually cameras will do the job for us, but we still have to go out there a hell of a lot. There's other nasties, too."

"Such as?"

"Decoys. Someone wanting to light up a train could send out a thousand falsies to trip the signal everywhere between Grand Forks and Fargo, distracting us so he can smoke it in Bismarck." He looked at the two officers. "This isn't a permanent solution, nothing is. These mass murderers will figure it out soon enough, and then we'll have to think of something new. Grand Forks is the largest rail center between Seattle and Detroit, so I've got a feeling we're going to be real busy." Captain Hall took off his glasses and the other two did the same. Ben was again surrounded by the hospital-looking white walls.

"We're lucky to have you on our side," and they shook hands. "When you're promoted to commissioner, Officer Porterfield, don't forget your friends."

A year later something new was a dire necessity, with false alarms and decoys popping up everywhere. They had been receiving sharp, clear signals, but whenever the cameras zeroed in, they found nothing. This had gone on for six months without a single attack, but everyone in the department knew they were being studied. There was much hatred in many places about a proposed formation of the North American States, a merger between the United States, seven Canadian provinces, and the Republic of Alaska. Grand Forks would be a ripe target for a small number of really twisted people on all sides of the issue. Some people howled that the votes had been rigged, others yelled about what they perceived as imperialism. Terrorism would make a major play here, oh yes! All team members worked exhausting double shifts on continuous seven day cycles. Stuck in the operations center, Ben was able to handle sixteen hours of work a day and six hours of sleep a night for the first few months, but after that it had harvested a good part of his spirit.

On June 14th, almost everyone in SWAT had been off chasing down alerts that could not be verified as being harmless, and tension was incredibly high. Someone obviously had deduced Ben's new invention and was now having a wonderful time messing with it. He and five others were manning SWAT headquarters alone. Neal Van Fossen had just returned from a false alarm. Neal was been Ben's age, a friend he had known since he

111

was an eighteen-year-old back in college. They'd entered the police on the same day and were both destined to advance very quickly. Neal was GOOD at the job and just never seemed to get tired, and to top it all off, he just exuded a positive spirit that really picked people up. Stress always just seemed to evaporate when this guy entered the room.

Ben and Neal had been first assigned as roommates in the plastic-walled, co-ed prison known as Stuart Hall at North Dakota State. Neal was a talky, six-foot-six, bragging jock who was there on a partial basketball scholarship, and at first seemed incapable of speaking of anyone other than himself. Ben definitely did not like him -he just seemed to have a feigned vanity about him, but over the next few weeks, Ben noticed that there was nothing fake about it. He also saw that Neal never, not once, demeaned, or tore anyone else down to make himself feel important; quite the opposite, he encouraged his peers to lift themselves up like he did, and feel great about themselves. Neal was also extremely fun and had a pronounced sense of humor. He laughed all the time at himself, and often at others, when he knew it wouldn't be taken hurtfully. Soon Ben realized, that Neal offered an openness and genuine friendship that he hadn't known. His own parents had always been about discipline; they were decent and never cruel, but had still been quite strict when he was growing up, enough so the he'd already determined that he would do things differently with his own family.

Sophomore year was really entertaining. Ben could always recall vividly about how his parents, the stern, never-smiling William and Jeanine Porterfield, popped in for a surprise visit on the day right after mid-terms, when Neal and he were preparing the third round of margaritas. Caught in the act, Ben said nothing, and Neal didn't really help when he offered a smiling, apologetic shrug and said,

"Well, at least this time we waited 'til after the exams for the drinks."

"Thank you for that, Neal, thank you so much," was Ben's answer in a pretty awkward moment. His parents were not in any way amused, but at least didn't say anything.

The senior year was the best for Ben and Neal, with the weekdays consisting of studying non-stop, but with Amy and Jesse, their girlfriends, the weekends were filled with roaring laughter, a little inexpensive travel to Gulf Coast beaches, and celebrating. It didn't seem like anything could put a damper on things, but then they realized that they were approaching graduation during a particularly severe economic recession, and the job offers completely absent. The only one of them to get anything was Amy, a plum assignment with an immediate promotion that also required her to relocate to a little over four light years from where they lived. Ben and Amy had gotten very close over a year and a half, and he always would always remember the sudden uncaring in her voice when she said,

"It's been fabulous, but my ship leaves in a week. Great knowing you," and that was the last he'd ever heard from her. Neal was more fortunate

113

in that he'd proposed to Jesse and she'd accepted. Right after graduation, when they were both hopelessly unemployed, Neal told him of his latest suggestion:

"I read a clip saying that the police are looking for hi-tech people, feds and state! North Dakota is making the choicest offer, so I'm going to apply." Ben could only shake his head.

"The pay isn't great."

"Come on, man, join up with me and the party will go on. Besides, it'll give you a chance for you to use that big head of yours for something more than supporting your hair." So now Ben Porterfield would start his career with the law.

Now, two years later, Neal's latest expedition had turned up a big zero.

"I guess we're lucky, Benstein," he said, walking up from behind him, "We haven't been hit with zip for an attack. Grand Forks: impenetrable wall of fortitude and valor!" It was a bizarre coincidence that he had uttered these words on this day. The alerts suddenly sounded on every computer in the large room, telling them with a scream that there was a problem just outside of town close to the birail.

"Cameras?" Neal asked. The corner of the computer screen formed a single box, providing an instant picture of a side of the birail housing. It was at a strange angle, looking down the length of the seemingly endless cylinder, with the ribs jabbing out in front. "See anyone?"

Ben shook his head. "No one, but look at that structure! They stick way out, and could hide an entire squad of people. Looks like you guys are off on another adventure and I'm going to be here relaxing on my butt alone."

Van Fossen grinned. "Not a chance, you're still a SWAT man. Sitting on your ass? Hell, that's what command is for!" He looked up at the glass office of Lieutenant Levinson, who had heard that. Their boss poked his head through the doorway, said nothing, and walked over to them. Ben looked at his commander with a sly smile.

"Hey, Lewey, can I go out and stretch the legs some?"

Levinson nodded. "You'd better get Nealy boy out of here quick so that I can move his desk into one of the bathroom stalls."

"Sweet! Field experience!" Neal yelled, pulling Ben to his feet.

The hover hopper vertically boosted off the roof of the station with its consignment of five officers plus one pilot. Ben fingered his weapon, a department-issued 4.25 millimeter Chambers pistol, and wasn't worried. He didn't have much field time, but did know how to use this all-important tool that had gotten him through basic training very well. He had also brought a wrist computer with him and was monitoring the signal continuously.

"They're still there and I got a bad feeling about this, guys. With some off-roader or a ball game gone wild, these signals usually only last for a couple of seconds. But these suggest some serious tampering." Neal pointed at several indicators.

"What about these?" he yelled over the whine of the engines.

"This has been going on for five minutes, and I'm sure the big one's a ticker. The smaller ones are lookouts, which tells me that nothing's ready yet." Ben thought about what he would do if he discovered one of those flat black devices on the rail. "If we find a charge attached to the housing, is anyone here certified to diffuse it?" All five of the others laughed and Neal slapped his back hard.

"Ben, we all are, including you!" Ben thought of those classes he'd taken: at the time he thought they were just to provide him with a simple introduction to explosives. *NOW CLASS, THIS -- IS--A--BOMB. THIS --IS--WHAT--A--BOMB-- DOES.* The secret seminars had been taught like a home economics course at a community college. He remembered them well, but never figured on having to use them. "Half way!" the pilot called back. *JESUS,* Ben thought, *WE'RE ORBITING, NOT JUST FLYING.* This hopper was quick. "Landing in five seconds!" The back door was angled down from the floor and spread across the entire aft fuselage. Ben had been last on, and would be first off.

And now Ben felt genuine fear. He donned body armor of heavy composite, not that it would do lots of good if a shaped charge incinerated him. Each man grabbed a pair of safety bars located on both sides of the troop compartment. They were decelerating and dropping fast, as the principle of the squad hopper was RAPID ATTACK! The large back door continued opening while they were still flying, and the driver was none too shy about

116

thumping the craft hard against the ground. Neal yelled,

"Out! Move!" He was very harsh sounding -it was the stress.

They were outside. There were so many supports along the sides of the structure, it was impossible to tell which one was hiding the enemy. Ben's coordinates were accurate, but they still had five or six of them to choose from. They were running quickly, and were all following him, as though they trusted that he knew exactly where to take them. By a terrible stroke of luck he did. Before he even came around one of the supports, he saw moving shadows. He stopped cold and each of the shadows very quickly changed into a full-fledged human being. ***THEY'RE STILL HERE!*** There were four terrorists in all, each dressed in a loose-fitting jump suit to facilitate speed and agility. They were armed, and had some lethal equipment! Instead of impact weapons, they had the full-blown military particle rifles slung in shoulder-fire positions, weapons that could slice through foot-thick steel instantly, like paper. Ben's actions were purely reflexive. He was looking at one of them down the glowing triple-dot sights of his Chambers. He yelled the script, the one he'd memorized two years earlier but had never used.

"GRAND FORKS POLICE DEPARTMENT, ALL WEAPONS TO THE GROUND AND HOLD YOUR HANDS STRAIGHT UP!" And then came a two-second delay. He stared into the eyes of one adversary. This man, maybe twenty, looked scared, but didn't drop his weapon! It was time to turn him

117

into a corpse, but Ben's finger was frozen. He couldn't breathe, and desperately tried to squeeze the trigger, but couldn't move. The muzzle of his enemy's rifle suddenly flashed a brilliant continuous light, unleashing a deafening, high-pitched shriek, like a power saw, but loud enough to rupture Ben's left eardrum. A bright fuzzy stream of particles traveling five-hundred thousand feet per second beamed over his shoulder. He felt the heat from the line of microscopic grains burning his face as they passed, and then heard what sounded like a bag of water burst behind him –a man had exploded- and he was suddenly drenched in warm liquid. Now shots were returned from behind him. Seven or eight or ten shots rang next to his head. He himself was about to pull back the trigger, when a second killer aimed the particle rifle right at him and fired, waist high. The glowing stream intersected where Ben was standing. *SHIT, THAT WAS CLOSE*. He looked down and saw the shining line moving inward from his lower right abdomen and disappearing in his body armor. The beam stopped tearing into him when the shooter suddenly had the top half of his head blown off by another officer's 4.25. Ben turned left, sending a tidal wave of blood through his blue suit. The upper half of his body rotated thirty degrees over his pelvis and legs that simply stood there.

OH MY GOD, I'M CUT IN HALF!

He fell forward and felt himself separating before he crashed face-first into the ground, listening to the thunderstorm of weapons fire overhead. The loud electric rippling of the particle

118

rifles and the "Crack!" of the impact pistols went on for four or five more seconds. He was losing everything when he heard a ghostly voice scream,

"Pilot, we've got men down!" Then he heard the loud "Frooom!" of the train rocketing past him, filled with comfortable and safe people, who weren't even aware of what had just transpired. Their lack of knowledge on this subject was their Heaven, and they would be delivered miles away in a matter of seconds. It was impossible, he knew, but Ben was on this train now. He noticed a very faint vibration being conducted from the floor to his legs. He was whole again. Through the window he observed a blur of surface features passing by at a rate of over two thousand miles an hour -they were far away from the scene of the battle already, and gaining distance fast. *THIS IS GOOD -THE LONGER I REMAIN ON THIS TRAIN, THE SAFER I'LL BE. NOW I'LL BE SAFE FOREVER.*

He awoke forty hours later in a bed with icy cold sheets wrapped around his legs. The ICU unit was devoid of cheer or the comfort of other humans nearby. He had a bandage wrapped around his head enclosing most of the left side. Thermal ultra-sonic shock had completely shattered his middle ear and it required two surgeries to have it re-built, but this wasn't what hurt the most. He looked under the sheets and stared at the perfectly transparent bandages that had reached up to his chest. There was a dark red, blotchy line starting at his right side and making its way to a point below the belly button. He hadn't been completely halved as he thought. The flesh had been cloned and fused very meticulously, and looked grotesque with its purple discontinuity against his pale white complexion. It felt as if someone had wrapped a red-hot steel cable around his him, and his eyes spat tears. The agony wasn't just at the surface either, it went completely *through* him, flowing all the way up to his brain, and more, his *Soul*. And then full memory hit him with the force of that train that had sped past him as he lay dying. This pain was *guilt*, making this jagged scar through his waistline feel like a mere rug burn by comparison. The torture of knowing he had the power to have prevented all of this if only he'd acted. But then he realized that if he had had an hour, he would still have had difficulty popping a 4.25 mm through someone's chest! *I SHOULD HAVE TOLD SOMEONE! I AM RESPONSIBLE FOR OFFICERS GETTING KILLED!* He tried to convince himself that he didn't know this about himself. *I'M SORRY, BUT I HAD NO KNOWLEDGE OF SUCH EVENTS TRANSPIRING IN MY SUBCONSCIOUS.* But in the back of his mind he knew and couldn't pretend otherwise. *ALL I NEEDED WAS A COUPLE OF POUNDS OF TIGGER PULL AND MY WHOLE WORLD WOULD HAVE BEEN SALVAGED. NOW MY LIFE IS NOTHING!*

There had been one officer killed, Corporal Neal Van Fossen. Two others, including himself, were wounded but would recover fully. Officer Geoffrey Stenson took a stream of particles in the shoulder, severing his arm, but the doctors were able to re-attach it, so that a whole limb would not have to be replaced. That's good, Ben thought. Limb replacement is horrendous. During the eight weeks Ben had spent in the hospital he'd been visited regularly by his mother and father, and once by his girlfriend, Lisa, who was to disappear from his life before he was even released. Then it was back to work.

Nothing was been reported to the news. The entire tragedy had been classified as Category 2 Top Secret because of the counter-terrorist technology involved, and no one would ever know what had really happened except for his unit and some medical staff. No charges were pressed against him, as hesitation to kill wasn't criminal neglect, in fact other police officers had it. But in this case it was surely costly, and had exacted the life his closest friend! That reservation ended the bantering with, and respect from his coworkers, and his career as he had expected it to be. Everyone would always now look at him as being the man who would not fire on the sociopaths, even after his friend had been executed. Lieutenant Levinson had always been professional toward him, but was never anything close to friendly after June 14th. Ben had been assigned to make refinements on the signal processor he invented, but it had become almost laughingly outmoded after the first year. He was never again assigned to a SWAT field mission.

A real darkness fell over him, inside and out. Red night would be around for two more weeks and the planet was bound to get a little chilly. The red star was hot enough to prevent Anteros from cooling off too much, but it definitely didn't add anything. It was time to get back to work, to return to Argo and warn its people about the tracks he'd discovered. He was still looking at several more hours to a very tiring workday. He thought of his impact pistol that still sat in his holster, and then his stomach acutely felt intense pain right on the scar. *WHAT'S THE POINT?* he asked himself. *WHAT IS THE GOGDDAMNED POINT? FOR THE LIFE OF ME I DON'T HAVE IT IN ME TO SHOOT ANYONE, NOT TO SAVE MY FRIENDS, OR PROBABLY EVEN JANICE.* The last time he had fired an impact pistol was five years ago to re-qualify for the field. *IT'S ALL ABOUT EITHER HAVING PERSONAL STRENGTH OR NOT HAVING IT. I DON'T.* He realized that it was unhealthy to dwell on something like this, and back on Earth he had seldom thought of it after teaming up with Janice. She'd helped him close a tragic chapter in his life, but there had always been a bookmark remaining. Now, lost on Anteros, he reopened the novel and, accidentally or deliberately, turned right to the page forbidden for him to ever experience again. This chapter was a page-burner, and he wasn't going to quit until finishing it.

Chapter 6: Repressions

The glow from Doctor Ervin's apartment window cast a solitary light across the main street in Treefall. Unlike any hospital on Earth or her near-by colonies, the clinic was very quiet after dark -one on-call physician, an RN, and EMT- since people weren't out as much getting perforated and lacerated by animals. Doctor Morahan and his wife lived in a tiny cabin on the outskirts of town, and Dean lived alone in a place above Koland's. Either one of them could walk from his front door to the ER in thirty seconds.

Dean always left his apartment door unlocked. He had told Ben once that he need never knock, so he didn't. He sat in the kitchen with his feet atop a large round table, his exhausted-looking arms drooping over the sides of the chair.

"You're still up?" Ben asked. Dean jumped. He had never seen the imperturbable Doc so tired. His eyes were red and wide when he turned and gave him a jerking glance.

"Ben. You startled me."

"Afraid I was that harlequin, returning to give the warden a little pay-back?" Dean tilted his head back and chuckled. He closed his eyes and Ben was sure he had almost fallen asleep right there.

"I let that cantankerous little fellow go this afternoon. He was starting to tire of my conversation -and his. My patients are recuperating nicely in the clinic, and my benefactor, the ever-stoical Kirk Morahan, has graciously conferred upon me twenty-four hours of off-time, starting an hour ago."

"You should get some sleep."

"I plan to, but first I'm waiting for one last experiment to finish fermenting." Ben shook his head.

"I thought you were kind of a flake at first, but you really are a hummingbird on amphetamines, aren't you?"

"I've never heard that analogy, but I guess it's accurate." Dean looked at a large satchel tucked underneath Ben's left arm. "What's that, a gift?" Ben approached and handed it to him. Dean quickly opened it and said, "Why Ben, you shouldn't have gone through the trouble -really" He held the bright white ivory up to the light. "Looks like mother nature won this round. Definitely a lemur. Old, I'd guess it was sitting outside for several years."

"A few weeks," Dean shook his head and said,

"Flesh decomposition is complete. Every morsel down to the molecule has been eaten away, and that takes time."

"I got it from one of the geologists at Argo. He said they found it in a pile of recent dung a month ago."

"A lot of calcium loss, I can tell that just by looking at it." He set it on the table. "I need to bring this to the lab to do a really comprehensive analysis. For now, I'm working on something that I've been practicing since I got here."

"I've got to go."

"Wait, you look tired. You look like more than that, it's been a full day for you." *SPIDERS,*

124

WASPS, AND UNSEEN MONSTERS STALKING ME FROM THE TREES, BUT I DON'T CONSIDER THAT TO BE OUT OF THE ORDINARY, Ben thought. "Just pull up a chair and kick back for a few minutes."

"When was the last time you slept, Dean?"

"Two days ago, but it's been a relaxing two days." There was a spigot protruding from metal jar next to the table. Dean held a glass under it and turned the valve. A foamy green liquid spurted into it and he handed it over. "I made this and would like an objective opinion. I was a home-brewing enthusiast back home, and what I've made here is what I think is a kind of IPA." The brew was as green as pine needles. Dean poured one for himself. "I think I'll only put down one. I'm not even on call for twelve more hours, but there still might be a real emergency." Ben took a drink. The last beer he'd had was over two years ago, a dark porter that reeked of chocolate. This was bitter and had a bit of alcohol, and was delicious! He took another long drink of a little bit of paradise.

Dean's phone rang. It was almost inaudible, buried underneath several stacks of paper on the table. He sprang upright and shuffled underneath the mess.

"Shoot. No telling who that is. Careless and stupid of me." He pulled it out and looked at the display. It had two messages, both from the safety office. He looked at Ben. "You?" Ben nodded, and Dean pressed the replay.

"This is an urgent priority message from Safety Officers Ben Porterfield and Scott Kubick, we have recently discovered evidence of a large potential predator near Treefall and Argo that has never been seen before. We believe that the threat is very high, so every person is advised not to travel at night. We also recommend that people travel in groups of three or more, with at least one member armed with an impact weapon. I would like to take in six deputies on a volunteer basis to patrol the perimeter of Treefall and to escort people living in subsidiary regions. Please contact the us at any time for questions. Thank you." Dean's jaw dropped.

"I went back to the safety office first thing and dispatched that message. It'll repeat itself every hour, so by now everyone in the Treefall area has caught wind of it."

"That's a serious smoke signal."

"Where there's smoke, there's fire, you know what I mean?"

"What animal could be worse than what we've already seen? I've heard rumors from some people from the Second that there's something exceptionally large, but so far, nothing more than nothing more than the knowns that's has ever been sighted. Did you see the anything?" Ben felt a twinge.

"No, but I found two footprints that were gigantic. It would take something that's really huge to push itself as deep down into the ground as this."

"Have you identified it?" Ben felt hot air blowing on him, mixed with a gentle spray of mucous droplets. That eerie, persistent feeling wasn't diminishing, it was getting worse. He pivoted his head to the left and right, and then up and down, a makeshift therapy he'd devised some hours ago, which helped a little.

"What's wrong?" Ben finished his beer quickly.

"Nothing. Just heed the warning. You're probably safe walking around in the center of town, but don't leave alone."

"What else?"

"Stay away from the willows."

"The honey willows? I heard that as long as you don't go on a marathon into one you're relatively safe. I know there are wasps that hang out in there, but they're deep inside."

"Don't even approach them. Right after you left Argo I saw what's in a willow from the inside the of an engine suit."

Dean smiled. "An engine suit! What an observation tool! Kind of like an aquarium in reverse. What did the willow look like inside?"

"Like a perfect picture of hell. You say wasps 'hang out' in there? They own the place! Plus there are thousands of spiders as large as hubcaps and they are just as bad as the wasps. There's a lot more inside those trees than you might think! And a few hours after I walked into that house of death, while driving back, I found a gouge in the foliage large enough to have been made by a bulldozer, only this was done by something with feet as large as a dinosaur's!" Ben hadn't realized it, but he was pretty angry.

"What else?"

"Nothing. That's it."

"You were talking about the willows. Scary stuff, and then you mentioned this huge gouge, which was even more frightening, and it sounded like you were leading up to the most terrifying thing of all. What is it?"

"I *felt* it! Something breathed on me, a pouring of body-warm air. I can still feel it crawling on my neck!"

"You obviously got out of there rather quickly,"

"And I ran like a madman. I completely lost it, lost my weapon, and flew out of there with my tail leading the way. This isn't open for discussion." And then there was silence. They sat there, neither drinking nor talking, for almost a minute.

"You say that your neck is bothering you. Are you sure you're not a few feet off?" Ben was impatient and was about to leave.

"I don't know what you mean."

"When you really exert yourself and get the adrenaline rushing, a large clone scar can sometimes act up. When you had mentioned your cloning work, I looked up your medical history after finishing with my two new clients. Not to be nosy, just to make sure that what you had was compatible with our equipment, in case of any later complications. It is, so not to worry, and problems this long after the original procedure are extremely rare. The file about your gastro-intestinal wound itself is cryptic, offering no details about how it came to be, just what precisely it was, and how it had been fixed. And then I remembered something that I saw a month ago, when I passed the hardware store and saw you in the back lot sawing a lot wood, I think you were helping out to build a new bridge for the one over Orson's that had washed out in an earlier rain."

"Yes, Terry and I had it up in a couple of days."

"And I noticed that you were wearing a pretty elaborate electronic-enhanced acoustical hearing protection. This is kind of thing that blocks out nearly every decibel, I mean complete silence, and is normally used by people working in air and space ports, or else they would be deafened in seconds. It had just struck me as odd that you were wearing so much for what you were doing."

"The noise from the tools can get pretty loud and it bothers me." Dean now looked very serious.

"I don't know how you were wounded, but have had some thoughts. I haven't seen you for any kind of medical reason yet, Ben, and I don't mean to seem intrusive, but can I talk to you as your doctor? Your doctor and your friend?"

"Yes on both counts." Ervin leaned forward in his chair and his face sank, looking very somber.

"Twelve years ago, after the U.S. Army concluded its operations in West Brazil, they asked me through the university hospital to research effects of ultra-high-energy magnetic micro-projectile wounds on people. Seventy percent of casualties who had been struck hadn't lived, but I conducted many interviews with people who did survive particle beam injuries from very close ranges. They'd come from many different backgrounds, and responded to their recoveries differently, but each and every one of them had one thing in common: they were all extremely uncomfortable, even fearful, around the sound of certain power tools. Not the tool itself, just the noise it made, particularly that from table saws and very high-frequency drills. Watching videos, I heard what a particle weapon sounds like, and I can understand why they felt this way." There was silence between the men, and it lasted -for quite a while- neither one saying anything. Then Dean asked, "Ben, is this how it is with you?"

Ben could only sit there for a little bit longer, fixating straight at the back of Dean's small computer sitting on his desk.

"It isn't just the tool. The memory is a combination of thoughts. It's the sound your own body makes and feels when these shrieking, seemingly infinitely fast ions move through you, a resonating, very deep hissing sound inside of you that really, really, just shakes you, and you feel it from your scalp to your feet. It's the feeling, very definitely in my case, that my entire top half had been severed, knowing that two feet of my small intestine have now exited my back and are hanging over me like a curtain, and then I fall to the ground knowing I'm done. Even when I was in the hospital, I just had this knowledge that some of me, everything that is me, had been cut away and lost forever. This is what the sound of that particular saw is like for me, Dean." Ervin could only stare at him for some time, at a loss for words. *GOD, THIS REALLY DID HAPPEN TO YOU!*

"I've interviewed twenty-four survivors from similar situations, and they all said the last part you spoke just now, some using nearly the exact same words. For years, all of them experienced what's termed as involuntary memory episodes -a very old generic term would be flashbacks, which is not descriptive of what someone has really gone through and feels, but do you also relive what's happened to you?"

"Sometimes, but nothing recent until several hours ago, and you're right, flashback doesn't begin to cover it. I don't only remember it, I'm there. I smell a weird lime deodorizer that one of our receptionists, Laura, had programmed into the AC unit when I walk into work that morning. It's not just a memory, I really am twenty-four again. This happened close to twenty years ago during a fire fight with some of those rail terrorists I was telling you about. That day my friend, Neal, had his head and entire upper torso disintegrated. Another friend, Jeff Stenson, got his arm cut off. I had been cut completely through, and this stream missed going through my spine only by a few millimeters. I was there for a couple of extra weeks because of intestinal complications."

"Upper G.I. wounds, especially in shearing, cutting action like what I've noticed on the report, can be a horrific experience."

"Dean, this was exceptionally painful in every respect. It's really striking to think that a simple mechanical motion on my part could have prevented all of it."

"Mechanical motion?" Dean asked. Ben formed his thumb into a hammer and his index finger into a barrel, and then dropped the hammer.

"That's a horrific experience, too. Have you ever done something like that before to someone?"

"No, not even with a stun gun. I was the police department's inventor, in a place where I just didn't belong one day."

"To be honest, I can't see you even getting into a fist fight, you're just not the type." Dean leaned back in his chair. "I could never hurt anyone. On Earth, I'd see nightmarish pictures from the image screen every night when I got home from work. 'THERE WAS A COMMUTER DESTROYED TODAY, KILLING ALL 450 PASSENGERS AND CREW ABOARD. THE GROUP **GOOD PEOPLE AGAINST ALL EVIL** HAVE CLAIMED RESPONSIBILITY.'" He looked at Ben's glass and continued. "You see, I don't see just people when I look down a crowded street, I see a mass of humans packed together, and my first thought that this is just a big crowd of unfamiliars. But then I think about how, in each person, there's an individual whom other people love and care about. And it's not just that person in the present I see. I see a young kid learning how to walk, learning how to eat and speak, learning arithmetic, etiquette and going on that first date." He set his glass on the table. "It had gotten to the point where I couldn't even turn on an imager anymore. Worse, I hated even to go outside. So you can see why I wound up on Anteros: me, a single guy with bright future in Virginia." Ben drank the entire glass of beer without letting it slide from his lips for a rest, then spoke.

"I had a more difficult lesson in learning I would have trouble pulling that trigger. People are decent, yes, but sometimes fighting is still necessary when they follow the really bad individuals. But I looked at this guy who was a kid aiming a rifle at me and saw the same things you see, and in my hesitation -my *cowardice*- a good friend of mine was turned into soup by a large-diameter particle spray, and the entire mission fell into chaos. I had always suspected that I would have problems unplugging someone, but did I tell anyone at work? No, I didn't. I could have told them about how I'd never fought anyone before and didn't know how I'd react, and they would have promptly kept me to the rear of the fighting. I didn't, because I was too damned afraid of what they would say and think about me."

"'Cowardice' is the wrong word for you Ben, I know you and it's just not who you are. I think a better one would be inexperienced, at least back then you were. Your reservation about killing someone is what makes you a good person. Someone without that kind of conscience is a monster. Cowardice? You treat that word as though it were static and unchanging."

"It's about character!" Ben shouted.

Dean shook his head. "Bravery is about being able to manage emotions like fear and panic. Every feeling needs management –I've seen people who'd been very 'courageous,' but weren't able to master anger, or personal insecurity, or envy, or any of a host of different thoughts that can be personally destructive in excess."

"My friend was literally swept out of existence because of my failure. That's not about controlling feelings, it's really serious shit!" Dean leaned forward in his chair and folded his hands together, looking, Ben felt, a little too clinical.

"Like I said, your records are incomplete, probably because the event and details had all received some classification rating. But from my own background, I'm quite certain that you'd been hit with a two or three-stage particle weapon that was at least in the five megawatt range. This is an infantry weapon that hadn't been designed for anti-personnel use, but for something much larger like cutting through heavy equipment or armored vehicles. The hospital where you'd received treatment was very thorough in repairing and healing your physical injury, but it seems to me as though they were very, well, remiss, in working with you to have a more…. a more across-the-board recovery. To be wounded with something like this is an exceptionally severe, traumatic event, and it's almost like they didn't even care about what something like this can do to a person." And now Ben stared straight at him.

"I deal with my own problems and don't push them on other people and make their lives miserable, too. And everyone associated with this – my doctors, nurses, co-workers- knew that what I'd done, or in this case had not done, had caused a fatal mission failure. Even if I had looked for more help, why the hell would they have cared?"

"Wouldn't you have?"

They both sat frozen with another very long silence. Ben felt as if his back was attached to a board –he'd never, not once, talked to anyone about this.

134

"Again, I don't mean to impose, but as your friend, I have to ask: does Janice know about this? I know you both; you treat each other with love and a closeness that I've never witnessed before, a very true kind of relationship that most people back home don't experience anymore in their entire lifetimes. But I also have the impression that sometimes you don't communicate with each other that well on certain very personal things." Ben grew fidgety. Memories of dating Janice fifteen years ago sprang into mind.

"A long time ago I spoke to her about how I'd been injured by someone with a particle weapon, but that really was it. All of the details, of me, of what had happened, I never mentioned, and won't because I need to work it out for myself, Dean. For most of my adult life I've kept this way in the back; well, current events have brought everything out again, for me at least, and I know that things have to be resolved. I may seem reserved, or secretive, but I'm not. I can fix this."

"You can't, though, not alone, not by yourself. I've talked to too many people in your situation who thought they could and it never worked out that way. You have someone in your life right now who most of these others didn't, and you can depend on her."

"God, Dean, I wish I could, but first I have to just figure everything out in my own mind before I share it with other people. I've now told you what happened, and I can work things out." Dean sat back a little in his seat.

"I know Janice pretty well at this point, three times as a patient, plus I've chatted with her many times when she's in town, and she loves to talk about her husband –*YOU*. She has told me, more than once, that you are everything to her, and how much she doesn't have the words to tell this to you. In this day, that is, well, that's something I don't hear often. She told me one day that you'd really been there for her during a very hard time back when you lived in North Dakota."

"I always will be there for her during any time."

"She and her older sister had been very close."

"Rachel and Janice grew up together, and were such good friends for all of their lives. They had recordings of the two of them doing everything from skiing at Copper Mountain to laughing together at our wedding. Even before I married Janice I'd gotten to know Rachel, and I considered her to be such a fun person to kick back with a glass of wine with. She wasn't just a sister-in-law to me, she was a real sister, the one I never had. She was just driving to work one morning, got hit, and it ended for her. It's been a little over ten years and I miss her, too."

"Janice was devastated by the accident, just absolutely destroyed. She told me that having you in her life at the time, with your understanding, your companionship, helped her get through it, to be able to recover and ultimately be happy again. She also said that without you, she would have gone through life without smiling or caring about anyone. This is what you mean to her. And what you are for her, she can be for you."

"She IS this for me, Dean, more than anyone else I've ever known. I think that ever since the first minute I've known her she has always been this to me. I don't block her out, or take her love and respect for granted, I cherish her! And I don't want the fact that I believe I'm a coward to diminish or erase how she feels about me."

"Ben, I guarantee that will never happen." Ben thought for a moment and then stood up.

"It's been nice talking with you, Dean," he said.

"Are you going to talk to her?" Ben could only offer a look that had nothing.

"I will, once I've worked everything out." Dean again folded his hands and looked down at the floor almost mournfully.

"I guess then we're going to be the only two people who know, then."

The walk from Dean's apartment to his light bike was not pleasant. Memories suddenly roared into his head from some black box, which he normally kept shut away in a mental vault, but now it was wide open. He kept hearing Janice's voice asking,

"Have you ever been hurt?"

Ben had never noticed what a beautiful view of Grand Forks that her place in Mittler had at night until now. It had stood very high and gave its occupants a glorious picture of the southern half of the city. The airport was in plain sight, with its dozens of landing squares and hoppers constantly taking off and landing, servicing a city that had become so large, it was the "Phoenix of the North." He was anything but surprised by her last question. With other women the conversation was always for general knowledge: what college did you go to? So, how long have you lived in Grand Forks? That sort of thing. But Janice had been asking him piercing questions all night, as she had every night for the four months that they'd been dating.

"What?" he asked.

"Have you ever been hurt in your job?" A recollection screamed, *GRAND FORKS POLICE DEPARTMENT, ALL WEAPONS TO THE GROUND AND HOLD YOUR HANDS STRAIGHT UP!*

"Yeah, four-and-a-half years ago I was hit with a ten megawatt particle discharge, and was burned through," he brought his hand from his side to his stomach, "from here to here. It missed my column, so I was lucky for that." Janice stared straight into him and then down at the floor. She'd never dealt with anything like this before and, her face was now covered with a very deep sadness.

"Benjamin, I'm so sorry for this. It's really hard for someone who's been through that to not think about it a lot, isn't it?" Ben stared at her. *NOT AN APPROPRIATE QUESTION.*

"Sometimes. I don't imagine it's anything you ever really get over. When it happened I didn't even feel actual pain at first. It was just a thin blade that passed through me like I was a ghost or something. The gun had been calibrated on a very narrow setting, and I guess I'm lucky for that, because a wider one would have just blown me up. It took

138

weeks of hospitalization and a lot of cloned bios to get me back on my feet."

"Do you have scars?"

"It's that thin white one that starts under my stomach and goes around me and over to my back on the right side that you've seen. It's not really even noticeable to most people unless I'm at the beach for a while or something."

"Why?"

"Because cloned skin may have normal pigment, but it doesn't tan as fast as the normal does."

"Does it ever hurt? Anywhere?"

JESUS! "Yes, sometimes a lot."

"Ben, I know you, now, and I really need for you to know that if ever…."

"Janice, I really don't want to talk about this." He walked to the chair and lifted his jacket. "I've got to go." Janice looked surprised and approached up to him.

"Well, I mean it's Saturday, Donna isn't here on the weekends, and you've been staying here on Saturdays." Ben gave her a look that had zero emotion (or so he'd thought).

"I think right now I'd just like a little time on my own." He kissed her. "I'll give you a call tomorrow and we'll figure out something to do." He left without saying anything else. *JANICE IS FANTASTIC,* Ben thought as he waited for the elevator. *BUT SHE'S TOO INTO THE PSYCHE AND WON'T STOP WITH THE INQUISITION. EVERY TIME WE GO OUT, SHE JUST DRILLS ON AND ON. I'M IN LOVE WITH HER, BUT*

***THIS WAS OUR LAST DATE. I WON'T CALL
HER AGAIN.***

Ben was hit by the worst memory of all just
before he mounted the bike. He had been alongside
the birail, looking at one of these would-be
murderers who had just installed a large explosive
device on the top of the cylinder. Ben's words,
***"GRAND FORKS POLICE DEPARTMENT, ALL
WEAPONS TO THE GROUND AND HOLD
YOUR HANDS STRAIGHT UP!"*** were etched in
his brain, but it wasn't even a real memory. He pried
and drilled at what had really happened, and finally
realized that in fact he hadn't said a word to him.
Ben had stared at the barrel pointed right at him,
and completely froze. His ordering him to drop his
weapon had been a wish that had never made it
from his speech center to his mouth. He wanted to
say it -to scream it, but simply stood there in
silence. ***MAYBE IF I JUST DON'T SHOOT,
EVERYTHING WILL BE OKAY. THESE GUYS
WILL SPARE MY LIFE. I'LL LET THEM
LEAVE, AND THEN DISARM THE BOMB.***

It was around 2500 hours when Ben
approached the house. He had phoned six hours
earlier that he would be very late, but the living
room light was still on.

"Still awake?" he mumbled, hoping that Janice
would be asleep. He wasn't in any mood to talk and
didn't want her standing there observing his facial
expressions for the next few hours, because these
ones were bad. He entered and immediately stood
inches from his love, who was waiting for him with
her smile. She stood on tip-toes and kissed him on

140

the lips as he leaned to her. Ben looked into her eyes, and after all the terrible feelings he had experienced today, her just being here was absolutely wonderful! It was as if he'd been stuck sitting in a sweltering, stuffy room all day, and now stepped outside into the crisp air. He held her tightly.

"I've missed you," he said.

"I've missed you, too. What's going on out there? You were in Argo all day and evening. I got your call and alerts saying that there's some animal out there. What's up?"

"I found its footprints, but didn't see what they belonged to. Listen, I've had a whole day's worth of bad times, getting educated on just how dangerous Anteros is. Do me a favor and don't go on any more journeys into the woods." Janice stared up at him, very concerned.

"What happened to you?"

"What do you mean?"

"You look different. You look really out of it and more than a little scared. Your eyes are strange and you're shaking so hard we might need to nail the furniture down. This hasn't just been a tiring day for you, it's been a truly hurtful one. Before going to sleep you should tell me what's on your mind." Ben didn't say anything, nor would he. "I can see it, your face is all tight and you're just not talking, and I can tell when you need to say something to me very badly." Ben recalled how he'd almost ended their relationship fifteen years ago. *GOD, WHAT A STUPID THING THAT WOULD HAVE BEEN!*

141

"I've got to get up early tomorrow and go back to Argo. Let's hold off." Usually, something like this did the trick.

"I would really like to talk to you RIGHT NOW," was her answer. Ben could only guess at how solemn his eyes looked as they stared into hers.

"Jan, back when we were first seeing each other I told you there were some subjects I didn't want to discuss. I'm feeling some of those things now."

Janice nodded. "Yes, and I understood. But we've been married for fourteen years!" Ben was outright surprised, she never pulled so hard at what was in his head. "I've respected your privacy and always will your feelings, but now we need to get some things out. You know every solitary detail about me, but there is this huge gap in your life that I don't know about. No more 'we'll talk later.' It just isn't right for either of us to just keep things away, because they'll keep coming back. You won't get better, only worse."

Ben shook his head. "I had a hard time in my life before I even met you, Janice. You've always led me away from it, and being with you is my escape. I don't want you a part of something that happened twenty years ago."

"And that's it, right? Twenty years ago, when you were shot and wounded." She was really determined. Ben locked his jaw in place, the muscles bulging through his cheeks. "You will never get over this if you don't share what's happened with the people in your life. To come to terms with something that has really shocked you, that still really frightens you, you need to accept

142

what has happened, as something that can't be changed and done over, learn from it, and move on. If you never let it out, it will build up and just absolutely wreck you, like it's doing to you right now in front of me." Ben slowly sat on the couch. Janice followed him, staring at him without taking her eyes off him for a second.

"I told you a long time ago that I'd been struck by a very high-energy weapon, the one that left this very significant rip on me. Well, nineteen years ago I was on a field mission for SWAT and stumbled onto a group of terrorists who had just rigged a bomb to a birail housing. I had to shoot one of them down, but I couldn't, and that's why I got cut with this spray. I really believed that I had told this guy to drop his weapon, but I'd completely seized up! I didn't say anything! First my friend, Neal, died, got everything above his middle chest blown out. I still didn't fire, and then I went down, and then another friend got torn apart. Three of the people we were fighting were killed, and I think that this entire disaster could have been stopped if I had just taken down the first person."

Janice nodded. "I understand. I know the anguish about needing to have done something differently but just didn't, to wish you had made one turn in your life, but made another instead. I do think that you've had some very unjust judgements made against you, from yourself and others, and that it has stayed with you. I have heard some of this before, Ben." He looked at her.

"Not from me."

143

"Sometimes from other people in the department. It wasn't like I was totally isolated from your workplace, you know."

Ben recalled an event three or four years ago, a formal dinner and awards ceremony. Successful attacks had reached a thirty-year-low and were still plummeting. The gathering had looked like some twentieth century prom night, with the men dressed in black tuxedos and their wives in sterling white – except for Janice Porterfield who, always needing to be starkly different, wore a very bright pink skirt and a tight-fitting red jacket. She was a real scene, and beyond stunning. Conversation had been polite if not particularly friendly, but when the men were standing separately from the women in a pose for a 3D, with their spouses watching from the other side of the room, Ben had seen something really upsetting. Officer Jeff Stenson's wife, a pretty blonde lady of thirty, was facing Janice, and spoke to her for several minutes. Her eyes were severe and her mouth unfriendly. She had told Janice something very unpleasant in a neutral, matter-of-fact way. Ben was forty feet away, but couldn't hear the words. And then Janice looked very offended, glaring at and Christine and spoke for half a minute, and then walked off.

Janice now kept her eyes on him. "What I love about you more than anything else is that you're a true gentleman. You don't want to tear people down, and found that out about yourself when you didn't expect to." Ben felt an avalanche triggered in his mind. It was a feeling of the usual guilt, multiplied by ten.

"It's not just that I was afraid of killing someone else, I was afraid for myself! My memories, my experiences, everything I knew being blasted away. I was never some noble guy who wouldn't raise a weapon against someone. I didn't want to start a fire fight because I didn't want to die!" They sat there, neither one looking at the other. "I'm nearly Forty-four years old, Jan, and I will not be over this when I'm eighty-four, or a hundred-and-twenty-four." Ben was terrified when he guessed at some of the feelings his only true love might now be having.

"I'm glad you told me this," she said, "and in a really tough problem like this you talk to your family, like we're doing now, and just work through it all. How are your now?"

"I have no idea. As important as you are to me, and my own life means to me, this memory really has boiled over and I can't let it go this time." They sat there for a moment.

"I love you and that will never change, and I have, well, since always. I really don't know what you were like before that awful day, but no single event can change someone's makeup. You're always decent, and always have been. I want so, so much for you to know that I am your closest friend, and that I only want to be here for you and talk to you and love you. I've always known that you're here for me, and that I can count on you."

"Right. Count on me for what?"

"To always be this thoughtful and valiant man, who would never do or say anything that could hurt me. To be able to sit around an outdoor fireplace with you and talk about a staff-and-flag game, or how certain alien animals resemble certain people we know." They both laughed.

"You're absolutely incredible, the best"

"I think so." Janice laughed. "But I'm telling you, Ben, I am genuinely afraid for you in this job, and if you get yourself hurt out there, well, then you're just going to have to live with some good ol' home cooking –my home cooking- until you recover." Ben held onto his smile. "And, speaking as your wife, if you think we're through talking about this because you're falling asleep, you're wrong. We still need to share our thoughts until we can put the past where it needs to be and just move on, okay? Believe me, please believe me that I need you."

"I'll always be with you, Janice, and I'll work this out."

"I know that we will, My Love." They slowly walked upstairs. It was the best night he had known in many years.

Chapter 7: Canopy World

It was different in the morning, still shaded like the day before, dominated by the noises belonging to those who thrived in the red night, but everything was a little brighter. He left the house smiling and rode to work not feeling crushed by the humidity for the first time since he'd landed. He was just in a much lighter mood. He had a wife who loved him no matter who he was. Last night was a bizarre finale to the second worst day of his existence, but the most severe day of his life had not yet arrived.

The safety office was crowded. Scott had never been much on conversation, but was an early riser and a hard worker. He was good at his job, and Ben's feelings toward him were starting to change. Scott had already taken in many volunteers, six men and four women. They wore their civilian clothes, but also dark blue baseball caps labeled SOA.

"And here's the commander-in-chief now!" he yelled over their chattering. "Got ten for you, Ben, ten more deputies." Ben smiled and looked into the crowd. He knew a few of them, like Dennis Thulson and his wife, Marie, a middle-aged couple in their early fifties who were the only experts in house construction left on the planet, and also Kim Koland was there, since she'd requested that Samantha, her fifteen-year-old daughter assume table duties, in exchange for more music. Kim had complained much about not having enough to do around her restaurant, and now she wore the blue cap. Ben had seen the rest of them around on occasion but only in passing.

147

"Glad to see you all. You received my warning last night, well, don't take it lightly. There was a disappearance reported yesterday up in Argo, and when I was flying back I stumbled across some animal tracks that could belong to something large enough to carry someone off. You know that people go missing regularly on Anteros, and no one knows why. What I need is for you people to provide two-person escorts for anyone outside of town who wants to travel. Always work in pairs. I also want hourly patrols around the perimeter of Treefall."

"What should we look for?"

"Look in the brush for anything, well..." Ben was about to say" out of the ordinary," but this whole planet was that! "Look for any kind of animal that you've never seen before that is big and menacing. Sorry, but that's the best I have right now, so don't go shooting up the place because of every wolf rat that scurries by or harlequin who wants to chat."

"What does this thing look like?"

"I don't know, but I'm sure it's there. Also, if you want a little friendly advice, stay very far away from willow trees. There's a lot more to them than meets the eye."

"But not the ear. I can hear those things singing and churning from half a mile away," Kim Koland said. Ben nodded.

"I've seen what does the churning up close. Please believe me and keep your distance." He looked his new squad over, making sure that everyone was wearing an impact pistol. "Okay, you've all got phones. When you're not making your

148

rounds or escorting, go about your business. If we need you, we'll call. Any questions?"

"What do we do when, if, we find something?"

"Don't shoot it unless it's threatening you or anyone else. Just call in and report it. We need information at this point so that we know what we're dealing with."

"Boss, I've worked out a schedule for all ten, if you want to look it over," Scott said.

"Just send to everyone." At that moment Ben's phone rang. He smiled at his new enlistees. "We really appreciate your help," he added.

"Hey, we're all surveyors. No problem." an unknown man said, as they moved toward the exit. Ben touched his phone.

"Porterfield?" A familiar voice asked.

"Yeah, Nate, how's the search going in Argo?"

"Still haven't found him. After you called me last night I went ahead and checked out those prints you told me about. I think I've seen them before, but not such sharp ones. I tracked them for maybe a quarter of a mile, and then realized how dumb it was to be there at night and alone. But I've never seen an Anteran animal big enough to squish into the surface like that." A thought hit Ben.

"What about up in the canopy?" There was a pause.

"You mean up in the trees? Can't say. We've never had the stuff to get up there. What're you thinking?"

"I'd like to see what's there. Not only that, but while aloft I could set up a scanner that would give us a much broader range for picking up locater-transmitters."

"That sounds fine, Porterfield, a real good idea, but to do this, you'll need some equipment. I mean, I think you probably have at least four hovers, the same number that had been issued to us, and they're all busted. What about yours?"

"We have four. These aren't like our bikes and still use turbines and stator blades. All of the moss and pollen overhead clogs these air intakes after about two seconds when they're flying, so none of them ever work. I don't even know how to fly the damn things anyhow, but all of our hovers are in the shop."

"Do you have any climbers in town? You know, mountain climbers?" Ben shrugged at the phone and looked at Scott.

"We've got Roger and Carrie Mattingley, a couple of experienced climbers, who've been everywhere from the Rockies to the Alps. Real pros," Scott yelled from across the room.

"Well, Officer Porterfield, you can come here later, but if you could get an antenna way up there to peek over the hills a little more, it'd really help out a lot," Nathan said.

"Before that, though, I'd like for you and the rest of the second survey to get what you need, bring what's necessary to protect yourselves, and come into town. I can have several deputies there while you do it. There are safety in numbers, and I think that all of us should be in one group."

There was a pause. "We already are in town, Ben: Argo. We all met earlier and agreed that this is our home and we're staying put."

"I guess if I said 'please,' it wouldn't do much."

"Even less than that, CSO," Nate answered, almost humorously. Ben threw a frustrated one-shouldered, hand-waving shrug to Scott.

"Alright, then. I'll get someone into the trees little later before nightfall. See you." He looked over at Scott and smiled. "So, Scott, how are you this morning? Well rested?"

"Yes."

"Glad to hear it. Have a big breakfast, too? I'll bet you've got lots of early morning energy that you're just dying to burn off."

Scott frowned a little. "Uhm, not really."

"Well, since I made you stay in town yesterday while I got to rove the country, I think that it's your turn to get a little fresh air."

"The air's a little too fresh for me that high up." Ben remembered Dean telling him that Scott had a severe fear of heights. No problem, he thought, *I JUST UNDERSTAND.* Besides, he had another task for Scott.

"Stay here, then. I'm going to give you a chance to use one of your seldom-used skills."

"Which one? I have many."

"Gunsmithing."

From the back room Ben returned with what looked like a large shoe box. It was made from wood, and this fact alone indicated there was some value for the contents. Scott simply sat at his desk, his eyes widening as though expecting some fantastic Christmas gift. Ben set it down in front of him.

"My favor to you is not asking you to go up into the trees, and yours to me is to do some work on something."

"You got it." Scott answered. Ben opened the box quickly and pulled out a long, black impact pistol with a ten-inch-long barrel.

"This is a Wesson Model 4200C, the first model of the 4.25 millimeter gun, and my dad was its original owner. He gave it to me when I'd graduated from SWAT."

"I've never seen wooden grips on a modern."

"Well, in high school and college I took a lot of woodshop. People always looked at me kinda funny when I registered for those classes of ancient art. It was a lot like taking alchemy or goldsmithing. My friends thought I was some kind of troll, but it'd helped with tuition money." He carefully rested the pistol in the box and slid it over to Scott. "I'd I like a trigger job, a straight, two-pound pull."

"One trigger job, check. Will there be a little something extra for me in my pay voucher for all of this?"

"No, but you'll have my undying gratitude." Scott sank back in his chair and gave him his usual look, which was nasty.

"Cool. Thanks."

For Roger and Carrie Mattingly, Anteros was a fine alternative to prison. They were both Smithsonian botanists like Janice. Roger, at fifty, was tall and a little grey, but was in better shape

152

than Ben had been in when he was twenty. Carrie was fourteen years younger than her husband and was as strong, probably stronger, than her spouse. Their bond was a wild passion for climbing that had taken them to some of the loneliest and remotest regions on Earth, but their favorite sport had been outlawed by most nations. Why countries had banned what many considered a religion, God only knew. In their living room was a two-foot-by-six-foot panoramic photograph of them standing against the background of a breathtaking expanse of thousand-foot–high cliffs. They were dressed in brightly-colored outfits, with Carrie wearing her long blonde hair in tightly-wound, uncomfortable-looking braids.

"We took this picture in the Kunlun Mountains," Carrie informed him, wearing a smirk as she delivered the punch line. "And we spent two weeks in a Federated Asian jail for it. Well worth it, though."

"Pretty tough punishment," Ben commented.

"Well, the first eight or nine times they only fined us a pretty penny, but I guess the Chinese authorities got a little sick of our flouting them."

"I'll bet that was the last time you went there."

"No, we got incarcerated for another two weeks when we were caught climbing there a year later," Roger trumpeted, receiving a rebellious "Hell yeah!" nod from his wife. Roger stepped over to Ben, holding a large picture pad.

"Here are the next adventures on our itinerary." Ben scrolled through the first few pages, which contained large color snaps of what looked like some ordinary desert mountains. They had all been taken from above, probably from a satellite, looking down on thousands and thousands of brown and lifeless hills. There was no green whatsoever, and no snow caps. Only one mountain range in the universe looked like this, and it was located on the infamous equatorial continent of Anteros.

"The Oreades?" Ben asked.

"You bet. These pics belie just how magnificent it is down there. These ridges that you see are really cliffs that are twenty-thousand feet high. The mountains are so tall, one wrong step in many areas can lead to a three or four mile fall. It's fantastic!"

"Just make sure you time it right." Ben thought of the Two-Year Terror.

"Of course."

"How are you going to get down there?"

"Hike. And once we reach the ocean, we'll have a very light-weight inflatable that's equipped with a motor as large as a radio, that can propel us across it in less than three days." *HIKE?* Ben thought. *DOWN THROUGH A THOUSAND MILES OF TROPICAL WILDERNESS, THEN BOAT ACROSS ANOTHER THOUSAND OF VIOLANT WATER, JUST TO GET TO A FEW MOUNTAINS? THESE PEOPLE ARE FANATICS, AND ARE JUST THE ONES I'M LOOKING FOR.*

"How would you like some practice? I dropped by today to ask a favor, and that's for you two to help me climb one of these pinnacles. I don't know how dangerous it's going to be up in the canopy,

154

folks," Ben said, folding his hands together. "But it sure looks like you two have been around and I could use your assistance." Roger and Carrie exchanged a grinning glance. This was a challenge for them, so he couldn't keep them away.

"We've been planning to go up one of those trees, Mister Porterfield, the highest we can find." Carrie said. "We were going to go up right after the sunlight gets back to normal, when Orpheus comes back out."

"Well, I'd rather head up a little sooner, like right now. I need to place a scanner up there, to make it easier to find people if they get lost or turn up missing, and I also want to just poke around and see what's living in the branches. Like I said, it might be pretty risky. Want to be deputies?"

"No, but I'll bring my gun if it doesn't weigh me down too much," Carrie said. She and her husband quickly walked out of the room to get their gear. This was absolute bliss for them.   All of the gargantuan pinnacles looked the same, since they could see only their trunks. Scott had met up with them right before they'd left. They flew their light bikes for two quick miles before Roger stopped in front of a tree and pointed.

"This is the tallest tree." It had a trunk diameter of around a hundred and thirty feet, and as Ben walked up to it, he felt like a caterpillar by comparison. The bark was perfectly smooth and glistened.

"Scott?" Ben called. "I'll get you a six of some pretty good local beer I was telling you about if you refrain from telling my wife what I'm up to."

Scott grinned. "I'm afraid it'll take a twelver for that, boss."

"I can swing that. I'm basically doing everything that Janice has warned me against, and she'd have some serious words with me if she knew I was up there." Roger approached, carrying a small backpack for Ben while wearing a much larger one himself.

"I'll be hauling most of the equipment. In here are some gloves and water that you'll need," he said. Ben pulled a small contraption off his light bike, a metallic scanner box with attachment clamps and a signal processor. He stuffed them into the pack.

"How exactly are we going to scale this thing?" he asked.

"You lucked out, Ben. We're going to use the easiest climbing method known, called stepping. We'll use these." Roger pulled from his backpack a packet of what looked like sheets of paper, eight inches long and six inches wide. It had a very abrasive surface to prevent slip. He slid out one that was perfectly straight. Ben held out his hand and Roger dropped it on his palm. This ultra-thin slab was more rigid than steel. Ben gripped its edges and tried to bend it, but couldn't deflect at all. The long side had two sharp prongs protruding from it. He reached for one of them, but Roger intervened.

"Stop. Those stickers can slide right through granite and wood, not to mention you. Take these grips." He handed Ben a pair of thin, bumpy gloves to put on. On the palms of each was a metallic ring small enough to fit around an index finger. Then

156

Ben noticed an equally-sized connecting ring, dangling from the metallic sheet he was holding.

"That's what I meant when I said we were going to step up the tree. We'll just push in these in as we go and climb it like a ladder. The tree bark is three feet thick and very strong, so everything will be fine. Have you ever stepped?" Rogers asked. Ben shook his head. "That's no problem. Carrie will go first, then you, and I'll bring up the rear. Just be sure to attach the ring on your glove into the ring on each step, because if you slip, you're dead. We're not hooked to each other, and we're going to be ascending to at least thirteen-hundred feet, maybe more. Mind if I ask you something?" Ben shrugged. "Why are you doing this?"

"There could be some real danger up there, and I'm not going to send you two up there to deal with it alone." Ben looked down at the grip of his 4.25-mm impact pistol and then back at Roger, who was now joined by Carrie. "I've got my four-and-a-quarter with me, so at least we're a little protected."

"Are you any good of a shot?" Carrie asked. Ben remembered back when he was in the police academy, how he'd been a better shot than his instructors.

"Yes." *WHEN I'M WILLING TO SHOOT, THAT IS.*

Carrie walked up to the trunk and plunged the first step in. Her hand didn't slow as the prongs impaled the bark, nor did she display any kind of physical strain. Just push it in, as simple as pushing a thumb tack through paper. Easy! She climbed onto the first step. It didn't move. She implanted a second, third, and fourth, all in a matter of seconds. By the time Ben walked up to the first ledge, Carrie was pressing in the eighth. That thick packet she held could have easily contained five hundred of them. Ben didn't have time to contemplate the danger of this climb until he was staring at that first platform, with Roger standing behind him nudging him forward.

"Let's go. Just ascend slow and steady, lock rings on every one, and you'll get there." Ben had never been afraid of at least the idea of ordinary rock climbing, but this was crazy! He mounted the first step, reached up, locked his ring on the third, and pulled his foot up to the second. Then he latched onto the fourth sheet and pulled himself up to the third, but he was slow. Roger called up to Carrie, who was ascending as though she was walking up-stairs, and asked her to slow down. Ben made it to the fifteenth step and looked down. He was thirty feet up. He could see the tops of shrubs and a stream running for several hundred feet. There was nothing to catch him if he fell. But with Roger behind him, there was no going back down -the slow way, anyhow.

He climbed faster and faster, clumsily linking his glove ring with each connector. He knew his motions were getting careless, but wanted to get this experience over with as soon as possible. Roger had cautioned him several times from below to be a little slower. Ben stopped after several minutes of furious work.

"Breather," he said, refusing to look down. He had to take these breaks every minute. They'd been climbing for over an hour-and-a-half and Ben's legs felt like balloons. He started to climb again, quickly losing himself in this purely mechanical activity until he heard Carrie say,

"We're starting to reach the real branches." Ben stopped, and saw up close the actual off-shoots of trees for the first time since he'd landed on Anteros. The horizontal wooden stalks sprouted out into the neighboring trees. Even these thinner subsidiary branches were thicker than most trees on Earth. He followed the gray bark of one, out and down. It divided into three more, with each one spreading out at least a dozen times before they became mixed in a tangle of wooden arms from other trees. And then he let his eyes drift straight down.

"This is too much," he moaned. He was eight-hundred feet off the ground. The surrounding trunks were now tall columns of wood extending so far down that they seemed to blend into each other. He had never known how much brighter the red sun was at this altitude until now. The surface was too dark to be seen from here, and the trees seemingly went down into some bottomless black void. The wooden pillars looked like they weren't even supported below --they could fall into that darkness and carry Ben down with them. It was at this point when Carrie spoke.

"Ben?"

Ben hesitated. "Yeah?"

"How are you with heights?"

"I never had a problem with them until now. If I had something more than a glove to hold me, I guess it wouldn't be so bad."

159

"Well, I'm going to continue this ascent at about a quarter as fast as I've been going, okay? You're getting dumb with the climbing, missing your ring, shuffling around on the steps like they were covered with soap. Want to go down?"

"No." Ben looked up. "I'll deal with it. This is one big tree."

Carrie smiled. "Probably the biggest in our known universe."

The first umbrella of branches threw a cascade of wood over Ben. He made it up to the bottom of the first, where the steps had been carefully placed in a spiral, around and up, disappearing over the top. Then he stopped for a break. He looked at the joint between the offshoot and the trunk and saw something peculiar, a cluster of spheres of different sizes attached to it, the largest being the size of a coconut. They were the same grayish color as the tree, and one could easily have mistaken them for woody outgrowths, but they looked too perfectly round. Fruit, he thought, some kind of gigantic nut. With his left hand securely fastened to the ring he reached out with his right and wrapped it around part of it and tugged. It wasn't held on too tightly and Ben plucked it off and brought it closer to his face. A perfect sphere, with a circular array of eight dark holes that were large enough for him to stick his thumb into. He'd assumed these had been burrowed by large insects treating themselves to a feast, but then the ball quivered and shifted in his hand. Something was still alive inside. One of the openings suddenly filled with a bony, toad-sized head with two eyes bulging out. A narrow, hook-shaped mouth opened widely and issued a loud gagging sound. Now the other holes were filled with --legs! Six short feet sprang out. Sharp claws from one of them dug into Ben's right hand.

"What the --get off!" The creature was screaming. From below Roger shouted, "Drop it or put it back!" The head retreated back into the hole for a second, sprang out three inches, and then pulled back inside. It moved in and out, each time releasing a cry and tightening its grip. This was a turtle, totally encased in a solid, spherical shell. Its six legs made it frightfully alien, five of them pivoting frantically against the air. So far, its claws hadn't perforated Ben's glove, but they were strong enough to feel like a very tight handshake. He waved his arm out. The turtle released itself, and was hurled away, but Ben had a new problem. He had thrown himself off balance, and then slipped off the narrow step and fell himself!

The glove on his left hand was still connected and Ben flopped back against the bark, and the ring, no thicker a fraction of a millimeter, was the only thing supporting him. He flailed helplessly and looked down into the abyss over nine-hundred feet straight down. The glove acted like a Chinese finger puzzle: the harder Ben's weight pulled on it, the tighter it wrapped itself around his hand. Carrie moved fast. Without connecting, she free-climbed down to Ben's step and tugged at his belt, guiding his feet back onto the artificial ledge. He stood frozen for several long seconds before looking over at Carrie, who stood right next to him, sharing the platform. She wasn't ringed, and only the grip of her fingers on the step above her prevented her from falling.

"Thank you. Secure yourself now." Ben said.

"Don't worry, I won't fall." Her confidence was bewildering. She stood on only several square inches of metal with no safety, but this didn't bother her at all. To top it all off, she gave him a lecture! "We've been observing these trees through hand scanners, and call that dude a tree tortoise. You'll find them up here by the thousands, usually nursing on sap at the junctions of big branches. We occasionally find some on the ground after they have fallen off. They're non-poisonous and totally harmless." Ben looked down, almost a little mournfully, and Carrie continued. "From what we can tell, they spend their entire lives crawling up one of these trees. That critter you shook off will hit the surface in about five minutes and may be a little pissed at having to start over." Ben gave her a confused look. "Oh, a fall like this isn't going to kill it, it's buoyant enough to slow down. I guess nature just built them that way." Still unsupported, she pointed up. "Let's go."

The top of the junction of arms formed a very wide plateau. It was kind of like being on top of a gigantic ball room, Ben thought. He could move his whole house up here and still have a larger yard than the one he'd had. The flat area was covered in moist, blue leaves, some large enough to use as a living room carpet. Further out, they intertwined with those intruding from the trees over. Branches rolled up the sides at steep angles, forming thick walls. The dense web of wood in between the trees looked strong enough to stand on. In fact, the maze of projections looked more like the ceiling of a spacious mansion, with leafy, wooden hallways and rooms going on forever.

"Amazing," Ben said, "This is an entirely new surface of Anteros. I'll bet you could walk completely around the planet and not even touch the ground. This is one reason why I came up here." Carrie tugged at his arm.

"We've got company."

Ben had seen one harlequin lemur, and thought that all of them looked identical to Hector. It was a misunderstanding, and now he saw his error. At first he saw nothing but dozens of eyes riddling the crevices all around them. When his sight got used to the darkness, he could very clearly make out those four-legged pelvises, each supporting a bald body of a lemur. The variety! Some were children, looking sort of like the large ones, except they were only one-third to one-fifth the size. There was a dwarf lemur around ten inches high, standing with the same posture as the adults and staring at him with a blank expression. Another was very large, standing over six feet tall. If it had stood straight up instead of stooping against its knees, it would have been two or three feet taller than Ben. Colors ranged from gray to black.

They gathered around the three humans. *THIS TIME, WE'RE THE ONE'S ON EXHIBIT*, Ben thought. The lemurs all held back a distance of twenty feet, no more, no less, some stood on top of each other, who were indifferent and uncaring about the weight. In all, there were at least a hundred

163

harlequins who had them surrounded. Roger leaned toward Ben and whispered,

"Don't talk." He sounded nervous. But Carrie smiled and looked at the spectators.

"Hello," she said. That's when the chorus began, of many Carries saying, "HELLO! HELLO! HELLO....." Each one sounded just like her. She frowned and stepped back. The talking was so loud it was like being in a small room packed with people jabbering their heads off. Roger threw up his arms.

"Now we'll never get those things to shut up!" Some of them began repeating this too, so it sounded like, "HELLO! HELLO! SHUTUP! HELLO! SHUTUP!" Even the youths were talking, and as far as Ben could tell, they were as proficient as the grown-ups at mimicking them.

"Let's just go. We can rest someplace else." Roger said.

Carrie pushed the step into a limb sticking nearly straight up. The lemurs, while keeping a good distance, followed, their tentacled feet dexterously wrapping around branches as they climbed. Some went up, from limb to limb, upside-down the entire way. Their equilibrium was extraordinary! Ben didn't want to leave, since these creatures were obviously trying to communicate with them. But the Second Anteran Survey had been here for ten years and looked at the lemurs as nothing more than pests instead of intelligent natives. Doubtless Nate and his crew must have tried to establish a dialogue, but had quit long ago. They ascended fifty more feet, but the lemurs were still below -it made Ben a little uncomfortable being stalked like this.

The pack of tree-dwellers stopped following them when the red light of the single sun Eurydice became very intense. They were closing in on the top bunch, and, just as the honey wasps stopped at a certain place from the trunk, so did these lemurs when they strayed too far from home. This meant only one thing: enemies above. Ben saw that some of the smaller lemurs --the juveniles-- still followed despite the refusal of their parents to continue. *RECKLESS,* he thought. Then they too stopped and reluctantly turned around.

"Almost to the top, Ben." It was now very bright and the chutes were much less dense. The thick web of leaves from the other trees grew thinner, but the tree Ben and his friends were climbing just went higher and higher. After another hundred feet the last of the covering divided and they chose this spot to rest.

The light from the crimson giant Eurydice was now a gleaming red. A couple of hundred feet above all the other trees, Ben looked down at the tops, but couldn't see through them! Horizontally, for as far as his eyes could see, they formed a blue and green prairie, looking every bit as solid as the ground. He had not seen such flatness since he'd left North Dakota. But there was something moving along this brand-new surface, and it wasn't a lemur. It ran on two legs, each maybe six feet long, and thinner than Ben's arms. A lanky body was supported by these limbs. Its torso and arms were very similar to the legs in width and length. It looked like a typical stick man drawn by children, but it was freely running along the treetops, as easily as Ben could skip along the ground.

"What is that?" he asked, pointing to this new animal as it swiftly passed underneath. Roger didn't answer, he just pulled out his tiny wrist recorder and aimed. This creature's appendages were so thin that it couldn't have weighed more than fifty or sixty pounds. Ben watched as it approached a wide opening in the surface, leading down into the dark abyss. He was sure that it would slow and go around, but instead it sped up! The opening was over a hundred yards across, and as it approached it spread its arms. Ben could make out a transparent web strung between its limbs and torso, and it sprang up with one tremendous bound. It hurled up and over the opening, gliding back down to the other side. Ben almost lost his breath and gasped,

"Whoa!" Carrie was astounded.

"It's just like a flying squirrel! Look at how fast it's going. I'll bet it's doing eighty." They were the first humans to see this creature, one especially adapted for living its life high above the surface.

They were up as far as they could go, sitting in the last of the outgrowths. The main trunk was tilted at a forty degree angle, and had been so for several hundred feet. The tops of the neighboring trees below looked as distant from them as the dark surface of Anteros had been when they reached the top of the understory an hour ago. There was a large clearing in the canopy, showing them the full fourteen hundred foot fall that awaited the careless. It was pitch black, and not even the mid-sections of the tree trunks could be made out. Ben unfolded the scanner and tested the power supply. He strapped it to the wood, wrapping a harness around it twice.

"We've got quite a view up here, Roger," Ben said.

"I can pick up every personal transmitter signal from Treefall. Now, I'll just type in some names." On the keyboard he typed in Janice Porterfield. The computer display showed him a very precise topographical map, and lit up where Janice was, about two hundred yards from their house. "That was easy. Okay, I'll type in Hudson Manley." The computer map shifted and rolled.

"Find him?" Roger asked. Ben's head sank.

"No. No damn blip at all." He looked for everyone else but got the same results.

When they made it back down to the village of the harlequin lemurs, Ben had expected to be swamped by its adoring masses. But as they walked out into the town square, it was deserted. There were no eyes peering out of the darkness at them.

Weird," Carrie quietly said. She walked forward and spoke, "Hello?" At first there was nothing, No friendly reply in her own voice, but then they heard a fluttering sound, a pair of wings. This quickly multiplied into thousands and thousands of fleeing birds. And then came a low-pitched roar, growing louder and louder until it shook the trees. It was an animal shrieking in anger or fear or hatred, and the concussion from the scream rattled Ben's ribcage. He covered his ears but that didn't help, and the shaking sound continued unabated. For over a solid minute

167

whatever creature made this noise had taken in no air. Ben turned to Roger, who had turned white in shock.

"Where did that come from, Ben?" This noise had been everywhere -to their left, right, above and below. They could hear something walking slowly inside the canopy with them.

"I've gotta see what's up here, so you two get down right now. I'll be down shortly, as soon as I get a visual of this thing."

"I don't think we'll be doing that. You're still a novice climber and we're the ones who brought you here. No way are we going to leave you," Roger said. And then another howling scream drowned out everything else. Ben plugged up his ears with fingers, but it was so loud that the pain dug into his brain. He could feel his teeth vibrating. After a while it faded.

"Let's get out of here. You two go down first and I'll be right behind you."

"I still think that you ought to be in the middle, Ben. You might run into trouble," Carrie cautioned.

"I'm going to be last because if whatever-the-hell's up here decides to come after us, I'll be in a good firing position. Go." Carrie and Roger stopped arguing and quickly descended down the side of the tree, leaving Ben alone. He looked down a dark passageway of wood. Sunlight pressed in here and there, but it was still difficult to see. Then he caught a glimpse something moving around about two-hundred feet away. It was large, a black mass that completely filled the corridor, and was moving toward him. Then he heard footsteps, the THUMP-

THUMP of a large two-legged animal. The sounds of footfalls came faster and faster, closer and closer. It was charging, and Ben almost flew to the edge of the tree, planted his foot on the first step and quickly disappeared over the side. He kept his eyes locked above him, not mindful of his feet sliding around on the steps as he retreated, but whatever had created that screeching sound wasn't continuing after him. After descending fifty steps, Ben realized that he'd not once locked his safety ring in place.

Chapter 8: Eyes

Ben had returned to the safety office and was preparing to call Argo when his phone rang.

"This is Dean Ervin." Ben smiled.

"Dean, what's up?"

"Ben, we need to talk immediately!" Dean sounded frightened, really scared. "I spectra-analyzed that skull and the findings are extremely peculiar." The office was quiet, with only Scott listening. "It was not decomposed by the usual microbes, Ben. It has been subjected to a veritable pool of digestive enzymes, almost as though it had been immersed in pepsin and hydrochloric acid! Decomposition occurred in hours, not months. There is nothing to suggest that smaller animals or insects even came near it, since there are no minute tooth marks. Ben, I believe you completely when you said that there's a big creature out there, because I'm sure that this lemur was digested by a single animal. Do you understand? The lemur's entire head was swallowed!"

Ben's phone suddenly beeped. It was coming from Argo and he had a feeling it was terrible news. He felt the sensation of sticky hot air returning to his neck.

"Can you write up a report for me? I need comprehensive information." Ben asked, suddenly feeling very dazed.

"It's already done. Listen, if there's anything you need from me, just ask, I've got a whole lab at your disposal."

"Thank you, Dean, but the best thing you can do is to stay in town and get ready for any casualties." Ben looked at Scott, who gave him a concerned, if not horrified look. Ben autodialed Argo. *GOOD GOD, I NEED A MENTAL BREAK.* The woman who answered in Argo sounded even worse than Ervin. Everyone except for her and her husband had vanished.

"They went out this morning, going in different directions, and no one called back. I've been on this planet for a quarter of my adult life but I'm as frightened as a child."

"Who exactly is left there?"

"My husband and me, Helen and Mark Simon. It's so dark out all the time now, and the woods sound different. We're barricaded in the equipment room. I'm looking at the trees and I can see something moving around."

"Could it be any of your team?" Ben was typing their names into the computer one by one, now hooked up to the scanner he'd planted a quarter of a mile up in the pinnacles. Their transponder signals had also disappeared.

"No. Its shadow is huge but we can't really see what it belongs to."

"Listen to me, do not go outside. I'll get on my light bike right now and will be there in twenty minutes, okay? "

"Yes."

"Arm yourselves, and don't go out the front door looking for anyone."

"Got it."

171

"Twenty minutes." Ben disconnected and walked through an open door behind Scott's desk to the storage room. He shuffled through several large crates and emerged holding something small. "According to our inventory, we've got twelve stun guns, ten now, since I've now taken two."

"Why do you carry a stun and a Chambers? A stunner doesn't do anything to animals here except piss them off."

"I don't know, I guess I just want to have lethal and non-lethal ways of fighting, an old habit. Anyhow, we also have twelve impact rifles twenty-four pistols." He reached down and touched the grip of his Chambers 4.25. "Like this one. Do we have anything that wasn't explicitly mentioned in our stores when we left Earth orbit?"

"Like what?"

"Something military, like higher-end photonic dischargers."

"Sure don't," Scott replied. Ben mumbled a quiet curse to himself. "I really interviewed people on the ship about this, same as you, and I guess no one figured on our needing to fight something that couldn't be taken out with an impact. That other stuff isn't part of normal provisions, but should be."

"I wish we had some, but a four-and-a-quarter'll do. Speaking of which, how's my Wesson?"

"Done. Only took a three hours, and I've given you a little bonus." Scott opened up his desk drawer. Ben noticed that Scott had respectfully placed the handgun on a very clean white cloth, as opposed to just laying it on a hard surface. He handed Ben the weapon by the receiver. "You've got your two pounder." Ben quickly verified this, checking the empty indicator light, aiming at a corner of the floor and lightly squeezing his finger. The break was perfect, like splitting glass.

"Keep going, boss. Pull the trigger to nine pounds." Ben pressed harder. He had never fired a pistol with a nine-pound trigger, and tried to keep in his mind that he was pressing the trigger, and not pulling it. Finally there was a second perfect "SNAP."

"The second puts your gun into full automatic, which will empty that fifty round magazine in two seconds. Have you ever fired a full-auto pistol?"

"No. We have the rifles that will do that."

"Those heavy Mark Twelves weigh over twenty pounds, and you're not going to be hauling one of those boat anchors everywhere you go. A pistol will always be there with you, but shooting it is a shocker at first, especially these higher-velocity impact pistols. There's so much muzzle flip that after the first twenty rounds, you'll be shooting at nothing but sky if you don't control it. Get some practice time with this so you learn how this thing acts in auto. There's also a feature that I've added onto the normal safety lever. You just move it one more notch further to enable, and the gun will fire automatic with the normal squeeze."

"I do need this. This is an emergency now, so I'll keep my Chambers, because I know the thing, and save the Wesson for when I learn how to use this auto feature. I'm moving on to Argo, and you heard those phone conversations I just had, so I'd

173

like you to do what you've been doing and keep coordinating escorts and guard Treefall."

"Ben, I really don't think you should be biking around alone out there. Want some company?" Ben smiled.

"I'd be lying if I said I wasn't about ready to jump through the roof. I wish you could come along, but I'd like you to stay in town and start bringing people in from the outer areas. There are folks who are scattered all over the place, and it's up to you to corral them."

"Sounds good to me."

Ben headed for the door. "See you."

"Take it real cautious, Ben."

Anteros had changed. The birds, animals, the noises between the trees sounded very different. The rats, with their orchestra of grinding, had disappeared, and the rain forest was no longer enslaved to the sounds of their incessant tooth-sharpening. But instead of the usual long whines of the birds there were short croaking noises. Ben listened as he mounted his light bike. *CHRIST. CRAZY SKY, RED NIGHT, TWO-YEAR TERRORS –THIS REALLY IS AN ALIEN WORLD!* If it were bereft of an atmosphere and life, and we were all confined to biodomes, at least it would be predictable. *THEN WE'D KNOW WHAT TO EXPECT, LIKE THE PEOPLE LIVING ON MARS OR CALLIOPE OR GANYMEDE DO.* He swiftly flew on his bike, and was turning into a light cycle professional. He knew exactly how much yaw and air pressure that was required to make turns that seemed to defy all of the laws of physics. Eurydice clung to the sky, poking its way through the canopy, its dimness still comparable to a sunset back on earth. He tried driving with his night vision on, and almost lost control. Too much confusion! All warm-blooded animals emit radiation in infrared, and in a jungle that was an ocean for his eyes to behold. When he clicked his visor on, every cubic inch around him burst to life. Everything was moving and he couldn't even see the trail over which he flew at seventy miles an hour. The surrounding flora appeared to be physically closing in to envelop him. No more of this, he thought.

The road had many craters scattered in it. Five miles out from Argo he stopped just short of a very deep pit that stretched halfway across. If he had driven over it, the air bubble beneath would have surely been ruptured and he would have wrecked. He carefully maneuvered around it and sped up. After a couple of hundred yards he rocketed past that mysterious gouge in the wall of foliage. Everything was red, but this dark discontinuity was still black. He felt the heat against his neck, and the dried mucous, impossible to wash off, and could feel his body physically shaking. He drove faster.

He knew there was something wrong when he approached the buildings. No lights were on and no one came rushing outside to greet him with frenzied relief. A thunder-less rain was dropping on him through the trees as he stepped onto the front porch of the town office, the Manuel Bradham Building. He tried the front door but it was locked. Walking around a corner he yelled,

"Hello! Safety Officer Porterfield!" There was no answer. No sounds of footsteps from inside, nothing. At that instant the rain turned into a downpour, almost as though it were deliberately timed to coincide with his turning another corner to see what should have been the back of the building, but it had been ripped away.

There was an enormous hole in the structure, its emptiness starkly contrasting with the interior light-blue panels. Ben approached, seeing that this tear in the structure stretched up to the second level, where part of the floor had also been sheared off. He turned on his night vision. The surrounding landscape was bright, oh yes! But the rip in the building was still black, a real absence of life inside. The visor didn't help him any further, so he turned it off and shined a flashlight inside. It was complete destruction. The floorboards were mangled and ripped away, exposing the muddy ground beneath. There weren't just lacerated pieces of wood, they had been pulverized into splinters. The panels that had formed the outside of the structure were strewn everywhere. He entered, first stooping down and shining the light into the 18 inch gap between the floor and the ground. A brief flash of the thermal visor revealed nothing alive lurking in there, but he found an impact pistol half-buried in the mud. He popped the magazine out. Each live round was symbolized on the back of the clip by a circular green dot, a vacancy by a red thirty-eight green dots: twelve shots fired.

He expected to find a couple of bodies, probably slumped a few feet away, and slowly panned the light across the supply room. No furniture remained intact. Tiny metallic parts and wire scintillated with reflections from his light. He recognized the components -capacitors, inductors, resistors. The sound of the rain crashing against the ground was tremendous; in fact, something could walk right up behind him and he wouldn't even hear it! He swung around and shined his light outside, but nothing was there, turned back around and that was when he saw the blood.

Liquid crimson was streaked across the far inside wall, as though an insane painter had thrown a fit with a paintbrush. There was a lot of blood and it was splashed in a straight line from the north wall to the south. Anyone who had lost this much could never survive. The floor revealed more pools, but no bodies, no clumps of severed flesh -nothing except a second pistol. Ben checked it, and this one had also been fired. Whether it had been discharged recently, or a year ago and never reloaded was impossible to tell, but the magazine was empty: fifty shots fired. A fight, Ben thought. The western half of the room, with its windows facing the woods, had been hit first by -something. It'd surprised them, maybe killed one, but the survivor made his or her last stand ten feet away. Even a novice shooter could press off three or four shots from an impact pistol in two seconds. This all had happened quickly.

The rest of the building hadn't been damaged, since Helen and Mark Simon had never made it out of the equipment room. Through the hole Ben could see the next building, which was just as baron as the

177

one he was standing in. He walked out through the hole and was hit by another disturbing thought: fifty shots, each 4.25 mm bullet white-hot and going four thousand FPS, had been fired three or four yards away at something large enough to remove the entire side from this edifice. It would have been impossible to miss! But the only spilled blood he found was human. The creature that besieged them had lost nothing in this fight.

He should go back to Treefall -that would be the most sensible line of action. He should go back to town, gather together Scott and half a dozen of his posse and return to Argo armed to the teeth. With Dennis and Marie Thulson watching over them from the rooftops, clutching their impact rifles, like Zeus guarding his mortals with his deadly thunderbolts, the rest of them could search every square inch of the surface in one large group. But Ben didn't do any of this. He looked at the row of trees in the distance, all a dismal shade of gray through the veneer of rainfall, and started off to investigate on his own. His computer had told him that the townsmen of Argo were all dead, he knew. Maybe the Argonauts had been eaten by some immense beast, and their ELTs were dissolved with them. Ben pushed on, needing to know. Voices shouted their arguments in his head, *THIS IS INSANITY!* Another spoke to him in a more rational tone: *I HAVE A LIFETIME OF COWARDICE, A RESUME OF RUNNING AWAY. IT'LL TAKE A LOT OF WORK, BUT NOW I'LL FINALLY SUCCEED. TAKE IT SLOW AND SENSIBLE –NO SENSE IN*

178

***PROVING I HAVE NO FEAR OF GRAVITY BY
JUMPING OFF A CLIFF- AND I'LL DO THIS.***
He saw movement in the trees! The torrents of rain
cast over him the optical illusion that the whole of
the forest was wavering, but there were separate,
distinct motions -shadows behind the trunks. Fear
bubbled inside of his abdomen and his white scar
started to throb. The rain was starting to let up as he
walked in a straight line straight toward the Astro-
space landing platform. The sheds, he thought, were
extremely solid. If there are any survivors, they
might have made it inside. He pressed on, and if he
encountered whatever demon had killed the
Argonauts or scared them away, ***SO MUCH THE
BETTER!***

It took half an hour to walk to all four corners
of the square. Each depot had remained unoccupied.
The outer lining was composed of pure inch-thick
titanomer, and no animal on this world would be
able to break through it. Once inside, Ben
approached the inner wall and pressed his magnetic
key ring against the receptacle and then touched his
thumb in the notch just above it. It was covered with
mud, so it took the computer longer to identify him.
A green light blinked on and he heard the electrical
ringing of the magnetic locks discontinue, and the
huge bolts moving off to the side. Ben noticed that
the red lighting inside matched perfectly the
sunlight. He entered, then closed the door and
locked it, and then searched all levels for one thing:
power.

The refrigerated compartments were located on
the basement floor. He wanted several large energy

storage capacitors, ordinarily used to trigger micro-fusion reactions in spacecraft. They remained superconducting at room temperature, but the ASR still stored them at temperatures below freezing. The icy air blowing on Ben's face from the freezer was pure heaven, and he stood there for half a minute savoring it. Then pulled out a drawer and reached in, lifted out a capacitor, which was the exact size and shape of a donut. It had two prongs protruding out of it, terminals for a simple electrical connection to a much larger apparatus. This was similar to the kind of battery you'd pop in a car, except that this one could probably light up an entire city for several hours. Ben thought about how the electrical generators had been destroyed in Argo, throwing the settlement into complete darkness. If such a thing happened in Treefall, there would be hundreds of people stumbling around in the dark shooting each other. This way, if the generators in town were knocked out, he could plug this capacitor into some kind of jury-rigged current divider, and turn the lights back on. He dropped it into a pouch slung from his left. He was going to play it safe, so he borrowed four more, sticking them in a pouch on hanging to his right. He was running up quite a tab with the N.A.S. Federal Government: now he was into them for five Global Electronics Model 24 capacitors and a space suit cleaning.

Without returning to the site of the Last Battle of the Argonauts, he climbed onto his bike and sped off. While racing along he almost forgot about the pit in the road, but he swerved up and around it with no small degree of agility. The air vents blasted the shrubs breasting the hole, as he rode up almost sideways. He was catapulted back across and had to angle the bike in the opposite direction to regain control.

"I just missed a twenty mile walk back to Treefall," he mumbled, *TWENTY MILES IN RED NIGHT!* He pressed on mile after mile, and then noticed something very disturbing -there were more gouges in the surrounding foliage, on both sides of the trail. Every half-mile or so he saw one. All of these strange doings began when the planet had gone into red night, Ben thought. He and all the others at Treefall had been trained to watch their backs during a regular dark night, when Anteros rotated away from both its suns. There wasn't anything particularly odd about this: some animals slept while others hunted, but they were essentially known entities. Red night was different. People disappeared, huge footprints had been punched into the planet, and most of the familiar critters that he knew went into hiding. This was almost a completely different world from the Anteros he had known. The planet had a red-night ecosystem!

He was several miles from home when his mind, tired of so many conjectures and possibilities, shut itself down. Now he flew down the trail at sixty, his eyes wandering from the left to the right. Then he noticed another void in the shrubs to his left, but there was something moving in it, and suddenly an entire wall rushed out at him. He heard a ferocious scream as he sped past, missing whatever that was by no more than a foot. Then the dim sunshine was gone, and darkness covered him. He turned and looked behind him -a suicidal move on a winding road like this one at this speed. The sunlight was completely drowned out by an enormous shapeless mass standing on the path. Its girth was wider than the trail, and its height -Ben looked forward. Another pit! This one was very deep and too close to avoid. The front end of the light bike dropped as though a thousand pound weight had been suddenly attached to it, and a wall of dirt came hurtling toward him and connected with the front of his vehicle. Ben felt the handlebars pressing against his ribs, harder and harder until they made a SNAP! His face smashed through the plastic windshield. He missed flying head-first into the side of the hole, an experience that would have broken his neck. Instead he slammed on his face against the trail, at a slight enough angle to encourage a slide that lasted for ten feet. He lay there for a several seconds, stunned. A stabbing pain was ringing through his chest like a bell, feeling as if something had impaled him. *THERE'S AN ANIMAL ON THE TRAIL, AS TALL A HOUSE, AND IT'S WALKING TOWARD ME!* He scrambled to his feet but lost his breath and doubled over -his lungs weren't working right. He stood up more carefully and looked down the path. The red night was back and whatever had made a grab for his neck back there was gone. He moved toward his bike, clutching the Chambers whose power supply hummed away. The cycle was crushed like an accordion against the side of the hole, but this wasn't what scared him. *THE*

182

HANDLEBARS AREN'T BROKEN! The "SNAP!" was a noise that had come from inside of himself, not the light bike.

His phone was smashed and town was going to be at least a forty-five minute walk. His broken ribs now sent a searing pain up his chest, but he could still move. He made his way toward the place where that creature had been standing, but there was no sign of it now. What first grabbed his attention were the footprints -huge and perfectly defined in a mold of mud. There were two of them, one on each side of the trail, sunk twelve inches into the ground! He looked up into the darkness on the side opposite from which the creature had emerged. In the past, when looking into these dark patches of shades, he could see some vestige of light penetrating down through the canopy, but this was different. It was as though a black wall was behind it. He saw nothing - except a white ball, and now two! They were suspended over twenty feet high and were a foot apart. They glowed, and Ben noticed that each one had a black spot right in the center. Then they both disappeared at once -just for a second, as if a light had been shining on them and blinked off and then back on. **BLINKED!** These two spheres, the size of softballs, were really a pair of eyes that had just blinked!

Ben's scar more than hurt, it felt that it had opened back up. He stumbled backwards and tripped, landing on his ass but keeping his weapon trained on the center of the hole. He heard the "CRACK!" of the discharge. CRACK! CRACK! CRACK! He expected this monster to rush out at

183

him. Maybe he could fire one or two more shots, but that would be it. CRACK! He heard something –tree bark disintegrating as the 4.25 mm bullet drilled into it. This enormous animal had shifted its position, and Ben could hear the grass four feet in front of him rustling. Still in a reclined position he pushed himself backward into the wall of plants opposite of the hole. Thin twigs and grass pushed over his head as he went completely off. His right hand clutched the handgun while his left was reaching and grasping behind him, holding him upright. It became very dark. And then his left arm was pulled out from under him.

He slid down a slope that was probably at a forty-five degree angle and very muddy. He continued to slide and his extended arm was the only thing that prevented him from somersaulting backwards. His right arm swung up and he accidentally squeezed the trigger, sending a bullet through the canopy and miles up into the sky. He skidded down to the bottom, a ride that lasted half a minute. He never took his eyes off the hilltop where he had sat before. The light down here was practically non-existent, but if that thing came flying over the top after him, he'd see it. It would look like a giant, featureless shadow but those eyes were tattooed on his mind forever, just as the 10 megawatts of dust had been branded onto his body. He glided to a stop. Nothing came over the hill looking for him, but there was a new problem: something moving and it was right behind him! He'd never before seen one, but he had landed right on top of a landmaster.

A lizard-like head emerged from behind him to his right, and he wrenched his eyes from the top of the hill to look down at it. That mouth with the fangs hooked inward -no doubt this belonged to a snake, and an angry one at that! Ben was still lying on part of it, he felt that much. It made a low-pitched animal growl and struck over Ben's chest at his left arm. He grabbed it, just below the head, having to drop his gun to grip its neck. It writhed ferociously, but Ben held it still enough to observe that it had no eyes! There was a large mouth with the long incisors and that was it. He tried to sit up, but from the bush behind him sprang another eyeless snake and another and another, both on his right side. *THEY'RE SWARMING, JUST LIKE THE SPIDERS DID!* Ben caught a second with his left hand. Two more emerged from the bushes, but he grabbed them before they could lash out. He had two fistfuls of screeching heads, but there was something very strange about their movements. When he pulled at the two of them in his right hand, he felt tension from the creatures in his left. He couldn't see where their ends terminated, but it was somewhere further down. Then he realized that these snakes were all connected!

A sharp pain struck his lower stomach. A fifth had bitten through his shirt and sank those teeth into his skin. He was helpless! He grappled with his four but that was all he could do. A sixth struck from the bush and buried itself into his right thigh, frighteningly close to his groin. And now Ben saw the landmaster in its entirety as he pulled it out. The beasts were connected, all right, to a large central bulb the size of a cantaloupe. The serpents all terminated along the lower side of it, so that they were more like tentacles with roaring mouths. They were radially distributed, and this landmaster looked grotesquely like an octopus, that had adapted itself to crawling over the land. It had six eyes, distributed every sixty degrees around its head. Each tentacle apparently caught living prey, shredded and swallowed it, and probably did a good part of the digesting, sending the nutrients back to its head and body. When one attacked, the other five were drawn into the fight, and the landmaster wasn't intimidated by a prey's size. Everything was symmetric about this thing! It had no front, back, left or right.

"Oh shit!" Ben cried, feeling the pain worsening on his leg. That mouth wasn't content just to have a good strong hold on him, it was biting harder and deeper. But he still couldn't let go of the other four. *THIS ENEMY IS ABSOLUTELY MEDUSAN, WHAT WOULD PERSEUS DO IN MY SHOES?* His impact pistol was on the ground, and there was no way to get it. He reached down and placed the palms of his hands against the landmaster's head and pushed it outward. Its arms became more vicious, but Ben pressed harder. The tentacles were stretched away from him. They still clamped down hard on his wounds, but couldn't dig in. The head was slimy, its skin and cartilage were mostly transparent. Even in this low light he could see its heart beating, its lungs moving back and forth, and its flexible bone structure. Further up, he could see its brain. Ben looked up the hill down which he'd slid into this problem. Great, he thought.

186

I AM TOTALLY INCAPACITATED AND INJURED. I CAN'T EVEN RUN! The only option was to walk back to town with this gigantic living parasite still attached to him, if he could.

He regained the trail after taking a very roundabout way back to avoid contacting some enormous and unknown beast, and the two miles which Ben traversed next was a journey through Hell, and more painful a tale than even Dante could have imagined. He had a landmaster gnawing at him in two places, and was helpless to prevent it, while an unseen demon that was several stories tall stalked him from behind the trees, never showing itself and never attacking, but forcing him to walk unceasingly against his terror and exhaustion. There was a very brief instance, just before he came into sight of the Treefall Clinic, he prayed his adversary clinging to him would release into him a lethal helping of poison that would end all the suffering in the universe.

Scott had been talking with Dean in the admitting room in the hospital when Ben entered. They had called him several times, with no answer. They were about to send out a search party when Ben tripped in, looking as if he'd been buried and then unearthed. He was drenched from head to toe in light gray soil, his face swollen and cut in many places and his clothes hanging onto him like rags - and something was hooked to him! They both wore shocked expressions when Ben approached.

"Jesus," Scott blurted, "what went on out there?" there was a squid attached to his thigh and stomach, with two tentacles tearing at him, and four

187

in Ben's hands. "Deano, we've gotta do something!" Ervin was already gone. He came back several seconds later with an RN and two EMTs pushing a gurney. Someone else gasped at the sight of a multi-legged animal digging into SO Porterfield.

"We'll be in ER. I want dermal pads of half a cc of dihydromorphine, two million units of penicillin, and 0.5 cc's of tetanus toxoid!" The two EMTs, a man and a woman, picked Ben off of his feet and laid him on the gurney. "I need two more people in here right now!" Dean shouted frantically. A deputy and an RN appeared.

"Doctor, what in the name of God is this thing?!" Scott yelled. Dean didn't look up.

"It's called a landmaster. I've read about them but never seen one until now." Scott pulled his impact pistol from its holster and powered it up. He pointed it at the landmaster, careful to make sure that once the bullet passed through this thing, it would run into the floor and not Ben.

"I guess we're lucky it's landmaster season."

Dean gave Scott a sharp glare. "Don't shoot it! Look at Ben's wounds, Scott. We don't know what kind of toxins are coursing around in this thing, and I don't want anything else getting into his system!" Scott lowered his weapon but kept it ready.

"So how do we get it off?!" Dean looked at his four assistants and nodded. They began to wheel him toward the pair of swinging doors.

"How's your hold, Ben?"

"Not good. These guys in my hands have been slowly wiggling out. If I get bit any more I won't be

188

able to hold onto them." They stopped in a large back room. Dean looked at the four aides.

"Okay, guys, you four are going to put on some of those X-ray protection gloves and then grab these –appendages- and hold them like a vice. Do not let go." Ben could feel one of the snakes slipping out of his fist faster and faster with every passing second.

"Could you please hurry the hell up?" he asked. He tried to act, and more importantly, feel calm, but was about to lose it. The EMTs and Scott disappeared for several seconds and emerged wearing heavy lead-lined gloves that went up to their elbows. They huddled over Ben, with Dean coaching them like a team captain. An RN's voice sounded,

"dihydromorphine, penicillin, and tetanus toxoid, Dean." Dean didn't pull his eyes from the snakes.

"Please administer when I tell you to," Each person reached down below Ben's clamped fists, and lightly touched each serpent but made no pulling motions. They looked up at Ervin for guidance.

"Okay, ready? Three-two-one-now!" The tension in Ben's fingers quadrupled. He panicked for a second before Dean said,

"Let go, Ben. Open your fingers." Everyone else held the serpents, but Dean still had to reach down and physically pry Ben's fingers open one-by-one. He looked up.

"Still got them all?"

"Got 'em," Scott answered. Dean looked at RN Debbie Stapleton.

189

"We'll need to run a full toxic analysis on his blood. From what I've heard landmasters don't have venom, but we must be certain. Admin the meds, please." The dermal pad taped to Ben's arm increased in pressure, feeling as if someone were poking him in his biceps; it was the medication finding its way to the blood vessels by permeating the flesh in a thousand tiny streams.

"People, hold the landmaster's head far away from Officer Porterfield without ripping its other two arms out."

"How are we going to get them off?" Scott asked. Dean turned to Debbie.

"Do we have 50 cc syringes?" Syringes were medieval, but most hospitals still stocked them.

"Yes."

"Good. Prepare one with pure morphine."

The transdermal pain killers really kicked Ben hard. His head fell back and dizziness swept him up in a maelstrom. He saw Doctor Ervin brandishing a large needle at him. *YOU'RE NOT GOING TO STICK ME WITH THAT JOUSTING LANCE, ARE YOU?* He was having trouble talking. The frantic words of the crew hovering over him became disjointed and lost their meaning. Dean did not use the morphine syringe on him, but on his predator. Ben heard Doc say,

"There it goes!" Dean held up that big, six-legged octopus-looking animal over him, its tentacles dangling lifelessly down. He saw Debbie reappear over him.

"We'll go over the entire list, starting with a scan of broken bones and torn muscles," Dean said.

Ben could feel himself being pushed away on the gurney.

"Wait, please," he mumbled. He saw Dean gesture to Stapleton and they halted. "Have something I need to say..."

"Go ahead. We have lots of time."

"Red night. There are new animals in red night." Ben had a feeling that no one would know what he was talking about, but Dean's eyes swelled and he looked very serious with belief. "The other people did not think about red animals." Dean looked up at the others. Ben said, "Red animals," one more time before losing consciousness.

Chapter 9: Redemption

He woke up fifteen hours later feeling as rigid as old wood. The first face he saw was Janice's. She looked ecstatic and had a very wide grin, her white teeth showing. Ben's first thoughts were sober.

"Don't go home, you need to stay in Treefall," Janice stood aside to let Ben see the four large bags filled with clothes and eating utensils slumped in the corner of the room.

"Scott came by yesterday and picked me up." Janice's face turned serious. "Bad things are happening, Ben."

"What?" Scott replaced Janice's position. Ben stirred to sit up, looking down at the bandages that were wrapped around his waist and chest, the sight of which sharpened some very bad memories.

"Take it slow, safety officer. You had four smashed ribs," Scott warned.

"What's happening out there?" Ben asked."

"Two more people have gone missing outside of town, and we've got another that doesn't answer the phone. There are around eighty people living outside Treefall, from half a mile to twenty miles away for some of the surveyors. The people further out are scared shitless and holed up. They're refusing to leave without at least a four-man armed escort!"

"What did you find?"

"The missing people had an empty house in very bad shape. Walls were gone, basement collapsed. We also found footprints identical to the ones you described. Whatever is out there, it's right outside the town."

Dean's voice broke in. "You said something about unusual animals before you went under. Could you elaborate?" Ben had to think for several seconds, his memory still a drug-laden jumble, then he nodded.

"When did people start disappearing? Red night! On Earth we were taught to be cautious at night, because many predators prey on victims after dark, a fact in cities as well as rain forests. But in this place there's also red night, a time when we need to be really, really careful, much more so than just a regular one. Hundreds of people have turned up missing over the years, most of the Second Anteran Survey, including those who built this hospital. I would bet that most of them disappeared just before or during a red night, when a whole different species of predators emerges from, I don't know, the trunks of trees, the canopy, wherever, and just preys on everything." Scott looked blank, not sure whether to believe this wild idea or not. "Listen to the forest! Listen to the rats or the birds! They're usually at it for twenty-five hours a day, but not during red night! It's all quiet. Creatures here know if they sing to attract a mate, they'll attract death. The natives of Anteros know a lot more about the place than we do."

"But humans and Anterans are mutually toxic," Scott returned. Ben cast a look at Dean Ervin, who was shaking his head.

"That is not always the case. Like I was telling Ben a little bit ago, there are animals here that can

193

digest anything. Up until now I thought that was just with some select smaller ones."

"So what line of action do we take? Evacuation? We have no surface-to-space capabilities, so we're stuck here for at least four more years!" Scott said.

"We cloister everyone together in town and learn like crazy how to live. The first thing we do is to round up everyone living in the outlying areas and drag them back if need be." Ben felt a sharp stinging sensation on both his thigh and stomach, a parting gift from his six-legged hitch-hiker. "There's no other alternative, and I'm going out right now to implement the plan." Three pairs of hands -Janice's, Dean's, and Scott's simultaneously landed on his shoulders and gently held him down. His ribs hurt so bad he wasn't in a position to fight.

"You'll be here for one more day, SO Porterfield," Dean dictated. "That's short for your injuries, and acoustic bone fusion usually takes twice that time, but after one more day you'll be at ninety-percent healed, and should be able to help rescue the stranded people. No less than twenty-four, though." Scott flashed a wide Neal-Van-Fossen-like-grin.

"No sweat, boss," he said. Ben nodded.

"You're in charge of the rescue, Scott. The travel-in-pairs requirement is still in effect, and also each person must carry an impact pistol at least. Be especially careful while travelling at night. A night that follows one of these red days is particularly hazardous. Get on the phone and tell everyone who's still outside of town to stay inside and out of

194

sight. If this creature sees them through a window, a wall isn't going to slow it at all. Tell the people to make for the front door when you call."

"Consider it done. I also found these capacitors in your bag. For emergencies?" Scott asked. Ben nodded and then slumped back against the pillow. "On the subject of impact pistols," Scott rested the maple box on a table to Ben's right, "I brought your Wesson. I figure you'll need every ace in the hole on this one."

"Appreciate it, Scott. I'll join you all soon. Also, I want you to travel with Phillip and Leona Englehorn. I know them and they could get lost in Southard Park," Ben said. Scott looked confused.

"I don't know Southard Park."

"I do. It's got five trees." Ben looked at Janice and smiled. "It has a hell of a fountain, though." Janice instantly remembered the days of Grand Forks, and Donna Baylor and her delinquent ex-boyfriend, hell-bent on taking that Oslo sports car for a cruise through that fountain. She cracked a brief smile, the same one that Ben had fallen in love with fifteen years ago.

Ben was exiting through the double front doors of the hospital when he was nearly stampeded by Scott, Dean, three other assistant safety officers, and an unknown man dressed in a black jump suit. They were pushing a gurney carrying another SOA with several white bandages wrapped around his waist and a bloody pad pressed against his side. Dean and two SOA's disappeared through the second set of doors leading to ER. The man dressed in black was Paul Ormiston, one of the residents living in the more distant regions. He immediately took to arguing loudly with Scott. Neither party even noticed Ben standing there.

"You see, we called you. I talked to you myself and told you we were coming!" Scott yelled, his face turning bright-red. Paul stepped forward, nose-to-nose with him.

"Then why didn't you come on the main trail?" Ben walked over and wedged himself in between them, sensing an impending fist fight.

"What's up?" he asked. They both looked up at him.

"Paul shot Phil Englehorn in the hip," Scott answered.

"I was defending myself. You weren't out there all night long listening to trees being ripped outa' the ground! You called us and said you were coming to take me and my wife back to town and almost immediately after that we heard weird noises coming from our back yard!"

"We got there half an hour later," said Scott. "And since we made the call from the Possons', it was faster for us to take a different trail. You're in town now, so you won't be needing that firearm." He held out his hand demandingly, but Paul made no attempt to give SOA Kubick his weapon.

"We'll figure this out later," Ben answered. "Paul, keep the gun, on the condition you don't go shooting at every little critter that comes strolling into Treefall.

"I agree." Scott now gave Ben a very irritated look.

"How's Phil doing?"

196

"Nothing too serious. The four-twenty-five poked a hole clean through him. Bone is shattered, but Dean'll fix that. We've still got other problems."

"Time?" Ben asked. Scott nodded.

"It's taken a lot more than we thought riding out to each house. We usually have to look around for the occupants once we get there, and after we find them we have to talk them out of trying to strap wheels on their residence so that they can drag all their possessions back to Treefall. We have fifty-four people in town, eighteen who are still out there, and those two confirmed missing have not been found."

Ben took a long blink. "Bad." He started to think that if he had assigned one SOA per group instead of two, those people might have been saved. *THE PEOPLE I NEEDED TO PROTECT MIGHT ALL BE SAFE NOW IN TREEFALL, WAITING THIS OUT!* He began to feel guilt. Scott held a computer in front of him, displaying a topographical map with bright red dots indicating where there were stranded colonists. Ben could see no reason why these people had chosen such isolated areas; Privacy is nice, but they had acted like hermits! They lived on the sides of mountains or way off the main trails, so no single road could get to more than one of their houses.

"We need to get everyone back here before the sun sets. It looks like each of these places will take an hour to get to and back from."

"You need to add one or two hours of messing-around-time," Scott growled. "It always takes longer than you think. We've got seven people including you. We've had a couple of SOA's take an early retirement." Scott meant that just as a figure of speech, Ben knew, but he felt it personally.

"You and I are in charge, Scott. You go with Leona Englehorn and Rosalie, and we'll send Dennis and Marie Thulson out on their own. They seem to know this place pretty well. I'll go with Steve Lewton." Ben pulled out an electronic pen and marked off which group would cover which areas. "Also," he added, "tell anyone else who wants early retirement that it's not a problem with us." Scott gave him a pained look and then nodded. They were off.

Steve Lewton, who rode a shaky twenty to thirty yards behind Ben, was the civil engineer who kept the water flowing in Treefall. He had never fired a weapon in his life, and Ben would have felt much safer if he had taken half an hour to show this forty-five year-old the rudiments of impact pistols. Steve seemed the last candidate to volunteer for duty, since his wife was exactly two weeks pregnant and needed him alive. I guess, Ben thought, protecting his future baby from becoming a late night snack is his motivation. At the first house, owned by Will and Linda Dalgleish, things couldn't have gone more smoothly. They each had one bag on their front porch, and their bikes were ready to go. That trip took all of forty-five minutes. The second rescue was a complete disaster. Eric Daneau was hiding in his basement and wouldn't answer the front door. Ben didn't want to just walk in, fearing that Eric would shoot him through the floor. They knocked for five minutes before Ben parked his light bike on the porch and jolted the two-by-fours with several loud blasts of hot air that sent the bike up three feet. Eric finally emerged carrying four times too many possessions that Ben could allow. Steve had proven to be Ben's diplomatic arm, taking only a minute to talk Daneau out of bringing his entire wardrobe and all of his electrical stuff.

They were on their last round, to pick up the O'Fallons, which was good because the dim red day was turning dark. The path forked, and at the intersection Ben could hear the whine of several bikes moving toward him very quickly. In the distance, the long trail going left was filled with moving, vibrating objects, a pack of bikes with Scott leading the way. In seconds five vehicles were parked in front of him. Scott looked very nervous, his usual sardonic sneer replaced with outright fear.

"Our last run, and there's something going on up there. We were helping these people load up when we heard these footsteps coming from the other side of the yard behind the trees, coming right at us. It was a damned giant! We could see this thing's shadow and I mean it was really huge! We dropped everything and bugged out."

"Did you see it?"

"I saw part of it," Leona answered.

"How tall?"

"Over twenty feet, maybe even thirty."

"Ben, this all happened three miles back and it was chasing us. If we hadn't had a two-hundred yard head start, it would have over-taken us before we got enough speed. It still might be coming, so it's time to go," Scott implored. "These two and the

O'Fallons are the last. That where you're headed?"
Ben and Steve nodded.

"We're going with you. If we stay in a larger group we may have a better chance," Scott said. Ben shook his head.

"What you need to do is get these two folks safely down into town. Steve, you up for this?"

"Certainly, Officer Porterfield."

"The O'Fallons are only ten minutes away. We'll be practically right behind you," The two people whom Scott and his deputy were escorting said nothing, revealing their genuine desire to tear out of there.

"I'll be expecting all four of you in half an hour. And don't go up there!" Scott said, pointing in the direction from which he came. They quickly sped forward and vanished. Steve looked with wide-eyed apprehension.

"I don't see anything."

"Don't worry about it," Ben said. "You'll get used to this." They pulled to the right and travelled down the second trail. *I'M NOT AFRAID, ANYMORE*, Ben thought.

The O'Fallons' house was large, with three floors and probably five or six bedrooms. It had been constructed five or six years earlier by people who, like them, had been planning on a big family, exceeding the NAS limit on kids by three or four. Unlike most of the Second Survey, these folks had survived long enough to turn over the keys over to them, before boarding the *Agenor* for the retreat back to Earth. The O'Fallons were in their middle thirties, and had learned that they could live completely out in the wilderness without having to forego a single luxury. Ben had always thought they were funny, with their big city-to-boonies materialistic attitudes. He didn't slow down when he approached. He rode off the trail onto the lawn and quickly circled the house. Steve followed, confused. They slowly came to the front porch and stopped. Ben waited for the electricity of his engine to die down before saying,

"I was making sure that all of the structure was still intact. At least now I'm sure that they're still alive."

"Structure intact?"

"I'll explain later."

Ben knocked hard and waited. There was no answer, but he could hear human clopping back and forth from somewhere inside. He gave Steve an irritated look and then opened the front door. The numbers of footsteps increased, sounding like there was a dance going on upstairs.

"Hello?" Ben called. There was a pause before a muffled female voice shouted,

"Upstairs!"

"Come on down and let's go!"

"Upstairs!" Ben slumped down in frustration and gestured for Steve to follow. The first flight of stairs took them to the second floor. They could still hear the frenzied foot-shuffling coming from above them. They rounded the bannister post and marched up to the third floor. Tom O'Fallon shouted,

"There it is!" As they emerged from the stairwell. The O'Fallons were huddled by the sun-fall window staring out through a pair of binoculars.

"Officers Porterfield and Lewton here to take you back to Treefall."

"Come over here and look at this, Porterfield!" Sandra shouted." It's out there just beyond the trees, and it is gargantuan." Tom handed him the binoculars, but Ben didn't put them up.

"I'll take a look, but you three get downstairs right now." Lewton gestured toward the stairwell, and the O'Fallons hurriedly went down. Steve looked back.

"You coming?"

"I'm going to take a quick scan so see if anything's going to pursue us. Get down to the bikes and get ready, and no matter what, stay with them." Lewton turned and went downstairs. Ben held the glasses up to his eyes and looked out through the window. He saw the faint black shadows of trees poking out of the darkening scenery, but nothing was moving. The road! He walked across the small room and glanced through the sunrise window, looking at the vegetation surrounding the path. The room was high above the ground, so if there was anything waiting to attack them on the trail, he'd be able to see it. He put down the glasses and looked with his bare eyes, seeing nothing threatening. He smiled and stepped back. ALL CLEAR. It was time to be over-cautious and take one last look to the sun-fall. He turned toward the window, but instead of seeing a reddened landscape, he saw black. In the center of this black field were two large eyes staring straight at him from only three feet away.

Now, Ben caught his first look at a gigantic creature whose appearance had always been obscured by the darkness. Its hemispherical head was wider than the window. Its face was very dark red or black, and covered with thick bony skin. But there was only one mouth, stretching beneath what looked like a long, bear-like muzzle. Ben was on the third floor, yet this creature was tall enough to stare him in the eyes. It had the ability to punch through that wall as if it were cardboard. *GUN -DRAW YOUR FIREARM!*

"Ben, what's going on?" Steve's voice called from the ground floor. Ben looked toward the door, then back at the window. The animal was gone, but its shadow revealed that it was moving toward the front of the house. In seconds Ben was rolling down the top flight. He smashed into the wall on the second floor, and threw himself over the last flight of stairs, not mindful about making sure his feet came into contact with the steps.

"Get out!" he shouted, approaching the ground floor. He lost his footing and grabbed the bannister, sliding down it for several steps before regaining his balance. Steve stood in the doorway at the front. "Take off! It's right here! It's standing ten feet away from you!"

"Oh my god!" Sandra screamed. Steve disappeared. Ben was at the front door when he saw Steve and the O'Fallons scrambling to mount their light bikes. The sunlight was completely gone, with only the windows along the front of the house providing what illumination there was.

From the porch Ben could see legs of this leviathan walking around the corner, each as thick as an oak tree. It had two knee joints on each leg, dividing it into thirds. Ben turned and saw Steve, Tom, and Sandra flying off on their cycles across the open field toward the trail. CRASH! Ben looked up and saw that the porch roof was gone -hurled away with one titanic swipe from the creature. Broken bits of wood and shingles rained down on Steve and the O'Fallons. Sandra and Steve were sent flying off, their bikes slowly hissing along now pilotless. They pulled themselves to their feet and limped after their vehicles, but they didn't stand a chance if this beast decided to hunt them. *THEY'RE DEPENDING ON ME! I HAVE TO SLOW IT DOWN!* Ben turned to face it.

Through the dusk he saw the creature staring straight down at him. Now it blew out a growl that turned into a high scream as loud as a jet engine blast. That long mouth was lined with huge teeth and could fit Ben inside of it completely. *THIS ISN'T WALKING INTO SOME DARK HOLE THAT'S BEEN TORN FROM THE RAIN FOREST, THIS IS REALLY IT –DEATH!* He reached for his pistol.

His feet were firmly planted to the boards as though nailed in place. He pulled his gun from its holster. For the first time in two decades he was looking down the front sight at his enemy. He didn't hesitate. *CRACK!* The monster didn't recoil, didn't issue any blood at all. The bullet was so tiny, he figured, it was nothing more than a bee sting. The creature unleashed another shriek that was so loud it literally rattled his eardrums. It tilted its huge head down, glaring at Ben with those two no-longer-anonymous eyeballs. And then it moved. One foot stepped onto the boardwalk porch. Beneath what was probably ten tons of weight, the wooden planks on the porch shattered and splintered with a loud *CRRRRRRUNCH! POP! POP!* A second foot smashed onto the floor and crushed more wood. And now Ben stepped forth, his feet carrying him toward the monster. He held the gun steadily with zero shake, aimed the sight at its middle torso, and he pressed the trigger. Four or five more shots in two seconds. Five more, and then five more shots. But he could do better, Scott had given him a bonus. He moved his right thumb up against the safety and pushed it forward as far as it would go, to full automatic. He gripped it with both hands and quickly leveled the sight between the shoulders of this titan-like predator and pressed down on the trigger. What followed was a continuous thunder, a *RRRRRRRRIP!* sound, the individual shots losing their distinction. The force was incredible. It felt like someone had thrown a lasso over the barrel and hurled it up toward the canopy. His ammunition mag was instantly emptied, having thrown out thirty rounds in two seconds, and that was when he saw his enemy waver, and just for a second it halted. With his left hand Ben swung up one of the spare magazines, which knocked the first empty magazine as it dropped out. The creature regained its strength

205

and rage, and advanced one more step, and so did Ben.

Now he was in range of the monster's gigantic reach. The creature raised its left arm high into the air. It had a circular hand with six stick-like digits that were each thicker than Ben's arms. He saw the shadows of these fingers whipping down toward him. At the end of each were scythe-like claws, each over a foot long. That hand was fast! Ben threw himself back, landed on his heels, and flew over backwards. He felt a rush of wind from this huge paw with all of its swords whistling inches from his face before it smashed into the front of the house. Laying on his back he saw the creature continuing to pivot on one leg, its arm digging deeply into the front of the structure. The wood -the whole front of the house became bent and contorted as though it was just a crumpled picture! This immense hand burrowed and gouged through the lumber, ripping out door and window frames and reinforcing beams and the living room ceiling. It finally left the building and swung up into the air, hurling thousands of broken pieces up and away. The entire front of building was gone, exposing the front rooms and overlying bedrooms as though they were part of a doll's house. Ben jumped to his feet when he saw that this huge hand was raised again, ready to strike him to the Eternity.

He flew off the deck and ran past his light bike. *NO TIME TO START UP THAT CYCLE, IT'LL BE ON TOP OF ME BEFORE I CAN EVEN GET SEATED.* He heard a crash which resembled the resounding "Crunch!" sound of an automobile accident, as this towering animal had swatted his vehicle high up and over his head. He kept running. Fifty yards in front of him his bike hit the ground upside-down and exploded. Steve and the O'Fallons were nowhere to be seen, they had escaped. He turned his head to look back. This creature was charging right at him and was already almost on him!

He reached the end of the small yard and was now surrounded by trees. He could hear the colossal feet of this monster pounding into the ground as it pursued. Ben compensated for his comparatively short stature by jerking himself suddenly to the left around a tree. *FINALLY, NOW I KNOW, AFTER FORTY-THREE YEARS, I NOW KNOW MYSELF. I HAVE FACED THE WORST OBJECT OF FEAR EVER IMAGINED, AND STAYED COOL.* When it had slashed away the roof, he didn't run, he stood there and guarded his friends' escape. He might be fleeing now, but only after he'd saved their lives. And then the images of his past now reappeared in his mind once again. Nineteen years ago he had fled from his guilt by withdrawing, by jumping a train that carried him off to a fantasy where nothing d time to activate their eight gigajoule bomb attached to the train housing. That detonation would have sent hundreds more men, women, and children to an airborne grave, but it never ever went wrong. He had been burned, almost cut in two. But also on that day, the terrorists hadn't happened, and his warning system was the reason why. And after nearly two decades of pain it had all become clear: this monster was both a physical being as well as an embodiment of these incredibly dark feelings of both his past and present. *IT'S TIME TO CONFRONT BOTH, TO TURN THIS LAST PAGE, TO READ THIS LAST SENTENCE. I HAVE TO DO THIS.* The monster was almost on him, so he darted to the left again. *I'VE LET MY MIND FALL INTO AN EMOTIONAL PURGATORY. NO! THAT WON'T HAPPEN! I WILL STAND AND FIGHT AND GET REDEMPTION, A NEED THAT IS A TORTURE INSIDE ME AND HAS LEFT ME STARVING FOR THIS LONG! TURN AROUND!*

He stopped and swung his pistol around, pouring shots into pure blackness. He could see the shadows of trees, and the giant was no longer there, but he could still hear it. He wasn't going to live for more than a minute. He now had had two lives: one of a horrific past and one of his life with Janice that was filled with so much caring, it couldn't be described. Until now he believed that he could reconcile the mistakes of his youth with some dazzling act of courage, after which he could revel in this love that they had always shared. But now he realized that if he stayed and fought this thing, he would die. It wasn't about having both redemption and love, a sequence, it was about having one or the other, a choice. Maybe he could dash back toward the O'Fallons' house and somehow escape, but he wasn't going to try. His decision was to stay. *THERE ARE NO MORE CHAPTERS. THIS IS MY LAST PARAGRAPH, MY LAST THOUGHTS, AND THIS IS MY END, BUT AT*

208

LEAST THIS TIME I'LL WORK EVERYTHING OUT!

"I also found these capacitors in your bag," he recalled his deputy saying back at the med clinic. He reached into his left pouch and found the fifth capacitor that Scott hadn't discovered. That much current would surely be formidable if connected to something, but he had no idea how to release that energy now. Then for the first time in several days he felt it again -that hot air against his neck. He turned suddenly and fired, but there was nothing behind him, and still, he felt the gushing wind. Now he realized it had never been coming from behind him, but above him! He looked up. The sky was drowned out by a shapeless black mass that had attached itself to a tree, its eyes shining out of the darkness from forty feet up. Ben pointed his gun, fired one CRACK! And then ran as fast as his strength allowed him from the trees toward a clearing. He turned and glanced back, but those two huge eyes were in pursuit. One second they were twenty feet away, and the next they hovered right over him. The monster had caught him!

A sharp blow ripped up against his right side had almost sent him flying out of his shoes. His feet left the ground and he was hurled backwards into the field. The creature didn't stop for a second -it came right at him again. Ben could hear the actual words of his mind's reflexes: *I'VE STILL GOT MY GUN. GOOD. RAISE MY ARM AND PRESS THE TRIGGER.* Except that the Wesson didn't fire. There was no muzzle flash or hard recoil bending his arm up and something was wrong. The action of moving his right hand up and squeezing the trigger had been only a thought -a wish. His arm was gone, just a four-inch stump of shredded flesh and torn clothing below his shoulder blade. Then he felt the pain from a deep cut, starting from just below his right knee, riding up his thigh, jumping up onto his side, and continuing all the way up to his shoulder. At the ends of his foe's dexterous fingers were those razor-sharp ivory hooks which must have inflicted the wound.

He didn't have time to comprehend the severity of his injuries. Those long, many-jointed fingers grabbed his legs. Ben tried to wiggle free, but his lower body had so many thick tentacles wrapped around it that he was completely immobilized as it lifted him higher and higher. What this beast had in mind Ben could only guess. *MAYBE IT WILL RIP ME TO PIECES RIGHT HERE, OR WILL IT SWALLOW ME WHOLE? WILL I FEEL IT'S ESOPHAGUS ENVELOPING MY ENTIRE BODY, FORCING ME FACE-FIRST DOWN INTO ITS STOMACH FULL OF ACID, OR WILL I LOSE CONCIOUSNESS SOONER? I HAVE TO FIGHT, TO RESIST!* He was raised up to almost thirty feet above the ground. *RESISTANCE!* That thought leaped into his mind and he reached into his right holster with his left hand and grabbed the stun gun, and then stuck it into the left pouch. He felt the capacitor, searched around for the two receptacles on it, placed the discharge lens of the stun gun against them, and fired. The creature's face was only three feet away when it was suddenly illuminated by the brightness.

It gave another terrifying howl that blew a hot wind into his face. The capacitor now glowed with a shining violet light and burned inside the bag. The neuro-electric stun beam had disrupted the smooth flow of electrical current in it and the result was a catastrophic, exponential build-up of resistance as all of the waves now interfered with each other. *ALL OF THIS ENERGY WILL BE RELEASED, AND I'M GOING TO DETONATE IT ONLY A FEW FEET AWAY. AT THIS RANGE, THE BLAST WILL TEAR ME APART*. Ben released the satchel from his belt *-GOOD! -* and threw it. The bag hit his enemy, but bounced off its shoulder and dropped to the ground. Then there was a brilliant flash of light, bright enough to illuminate the entire rain forest for miles around, blinding Ben, followed by a thundering **WHOOOM!!** that completely blew out his hearing. Only his tactile sense remained, and he felt a rush of wind against his skin, first in the direction from his feet to his head, and then his stomach to his back -he was falling. He landed front-first on something hard, and then there was nothing.

Everything was a pure, beautiful white. But then weight and darkness pulled him into the world. The black shades of night came down on his reality like a curtain over a brightly lit stage. The two-foot-thick grass he'd landed on saved him from breaking every bone, but he felt a pain ripping at him, an agony he hadn't felt even when he'd almost been sliced in half many years ago. Pallor hung right above him in the sky, poking through the canopy and faintly lighting the small meadow in which he

211

was sprawled. There was white everywhere -not a light source, but blotches. By the way the cream pigment scintillated in the moonlight, with its glossy texture, Ben could tell it was wet. He limped over to one white mass covering an area of many tarpaulins, leaned over, and stuck his last-remaining index finger in it. Warm! It was hot, maybe ten or twenty degrees hotter than his own body temperature. He remembered learning about blood: red blood contained iron, white blood had nickel. The mammoth image of his enemy filled his mind, remembering its scream when the capacitor had burst right next to its leg. It must have dropped him, and then rushed out of there, carving a trail for itself in the brush which the white blood verified and the moonlight confirmed.

Ben pulled himself down the trail. He found his pistol, -wasn't good at shooting left-handed, but would learn- and that would more than do. *DO WHAT?* He asked. *REDEMPTION. THE MONSTER'S WOUNDED, AND I'LL BE ABLE TO CATCH IT AND FINALLY WIN. NO MORE RETREATING. I'LL PROVE MYSELF TO JAN AND LENVISONON AND THE DEPARTMENT AND TO MYSELF. I'LL GET THIS OFF MY SOUL ONCE AND FOR ONCE AND FOR ALL AND THEN I CAN REALLY LOVE JANICE.* He felt a third as strong as usual, and had lost his arm! It may have been his imagination, but he thought he heard his blood running out of his wound and falling to the ground. Ben's eyes scanned left and right, but the trail of white blood went straight ahead forever. *THE SITUATION HASN'T*

212

CHANGED. I'LL TRACK AND KILL THIS PREDATOR EVEN IF IT MEANS LOSING EVERY DROP OF BLOOD FROM MY BODY AND I'M JUST A CORPSE TO BE CONSUMED BY THE BEETLES, BECAUSE, GODDAMMIT, THIS IS SOMETHING THAT REALLY MATTERS! But now a conscience inside of him that had been screaming at him through a sound-proof enclosure was now loudly heard, a voice from whom he used to be: a loving husband to Janice, and a kind and gentle friend to everyone who had ever known him. *I CAN'T LEAVE LIKE THIS! YEARS OF GUILT AND PAIN -WHY? I AM WITH A WOMAN WHO WANTS ONLY TO SPEND HER LIFE WITH ME, TO SHARE HER SOUL WITH MINE. AND DESPITE EVERYTHING JANICE MEANS TO ME, I'VE GIVEN HER UP FOR MY OWN REDEMPTION. EVERYONE IN MY LIFE I'VE DESERTED. IT ISN'T VINDICATION I'M NOW SEEKING, IT'S SUICIDE!*

He fell forward, but caught himself with his hand, stopping his face from hitting the ground and stared straight down. Now he understood his strange monthly dream, with people dancing about as shadows and singing: he himself had always been the fading shadow, no one else, in the midst of people he loved or who had ever loved him, unable to truly see them or hear their cries because he'd muted their voices in a refusal to listen. He now knew that they were *PLEADING* with him, *DON'T SACRAFICE YOURSELF! DON'T DIE! WE NEED YOU!* He finally called out to them, *AND I*

NEED YOU! Now he knew that the man he truly needed to be was one he'd always been. He'd thought he found himself earlier, but now he really had.

He was limping home, but had no memory of ever having climbed to his feet. He used some of the torn sleeve material on his right side to make a tourniquet with which he could twist around the severed flesh of what had been an arm and clamp it tightly closed. He barely made it back onto the lawn of the O'Fallons. There were light bikes and a medical transport parked outside. He could hear people talking, searching in different directions but they didn't see him. He slowly moved onto what remained of the shattered porch and then through the massive hole in the front of the house. He saw SOA Leona Englehorn, Scott, and Janice standing in the center of the living room. They had been talking when they saw him. Their eyes revealed to Ben the horror of his injuries. He had never seen Janice so panicked.

"Ben -" she started. Ben's right leg finally buckled and he slowly tipped over sideways. All three rushed to him, catching him and easing his fall against the floor.

"I'll get Doctor Ervin," Leona called, running to the front of the house. Janice moved quickly: she ripped the sleeve off Ben's shirt, revealing an absent arm and blood pouring out of the wound. She grabbed what was left, stopped the rush of blood, and prevented him from bleeding to death right there. Her hands were trembling like he'd never

214

seen or felt. Dean appeared over him, looking very, very afraid.

"God, keep holding on, Janice, he's very pale, in deep shock, really struggling." He looked up at Scott and more two EMTs and tried to talk quietly, but Ben heard every word. "Get the crash kit and heavy plasma supply against the wall there, he's about to code. You folks, let's get him wrapped." Scott ran across the room, and Dean worked quickly with Jan and the medical technicians to stop the bleeding from the stump and all along his side right side with bandages.

"Everything is okay, Ben, but I need for you to stay awake and talk to us, just keep your eyes open so we can get you stabilized. Please, just keep talking." Janice worked with their doctor, and then she caught Ben in a stare with her incredible green eyes before saying,

"You did it again, Ben. You came through for people. I don't know how I can say more strongly that you've always been my inspiration, my most incredible partner, and have been since the first time I talked to you. I just want you to know that I love you and will always be here. I want you to revel in *OUR* life, too. If that's on Earth, I'll fly back there with you. Where-ever you are, I will always be there next to you."

Ben knew that everyone *NOW* were people who truly moved him in life, and hadn't even realized this until his own was about to stop. Janice, his wife, and Dean Ervin, his closest friends, *THESE ARE PEOPLE WHO ARE WITH ME!* He couldn't touch the past, and it was there to stay.

215

Benjamin Porterfield: incompetent coward, whose friend lost his life because of his ineffectual response in a death-struggle; Benjamin Porterfield: hero, whose idea two decades ago had saved many hundreds if not thousands of lives, and who'd now single-handedly braved a predatory titan so that three others might escape and live. He had found his life four hundred light years from where he was born, and would not have to endure its trials alone. He looked up into Janice's eyes, and felt his new-found world, an awakening after a long dream.

"Janice, I love you. I've really had some awful times, and let them move my feelings away from everything that matters to me now, but I want so much to live and spend every second with you, and I will not suffocate in nightmares anymore. My Love, this is my Redemption: I'll always come home and be there for you, and for myself."

Chapter 10: Anteros

Ben Porterfield lived on the new world for fifty-eight more years, and Janice for two years longer. It had proven to be an entirely new existence for them, but it still helped them understand the place from which they came. Their pasts were experiences to be learned from, not drowned in, and any memory or feeling was something that could be lived with and understood. Their three children, each with a propensity for trouble, left them with little time for reflection. They now knew how to survive in a new reality and live with the old.

Rachel Schiller came by every day to see Dean Ervin, the painter. "The Doc" had been retired for ten years and since his wife, Karen, had passed away three years ago, he'd spent most of his time inside his cabin on the outskirts of town. Rachel often had to wait for several minutes after knocking; Dean was getting slower every year and his hearing, despite numerous operations, it was almost gone. He appeared in the doorway, dressed in a dark gray smock that was covered with brush marks of oil paint of every different color. Up until several years ago he'd kept his hair pitch black, but now, at a hundred and fifteen years of age, he had let it explode in what looked like a pure white bush.

"You started out as my pupil and wound up retiring me," Dean griped. They sat at one of the fifteen outdoor tables in front of Koland's. Rachel was fifty-one, and Dean had often commented about how she looked very much like her mother, Janice, did many years ago, except that Rachel preferred to keep her light brown hair shoulder-length and straight.

"You were a hundred and five. We at the hospital figured you might want to try something else." Doctor Schiller had recently been promoted to chief of surgery.

"What do you think of my latest scribbling?" Dean thought about the mass of green, blue and black laid out on canvass back in his home. "No one paints anymore. It's all done on computers. I figure I'll work my way up to that, once I get the hang of painting."

"Don't change a thing, Dean, it looks magnificent."

"Hardly. I'm a terrible painter, but I'm getting better every year. That's what's important, not just reaching the goal, but the fight to get there." He pushed forward his hand and grabbed a saltshaker, sprinkling it on his lunch. "I'm always improving, in my prime right now."

The sky was growing dim.

"Red night," Rachel said. Dean looked at her, since for a second he was living decades ago and looking at one of his best friends, Janice, who'd spoken those exact words, *Red night!* Up in the sky Orpheus was parked right next to Eurydice, and in a few moments it would hide once more for two weeks. The two thousand occupants of Treefall were coming into town. A group of half a dozen children, all under ten, were galloping and screaming down the road, were playing a game of howler tag. Dean smiled.

218

"It's so strange to see people running around whom I didn't deliver or see delivered. It's like they're always going to be strangers to me."

"Well, you'll never be a stranger to me," Rachel said with a smile. Dean had delivered her and her two older brothers.

"Where are Neal and Andy, anyhow? Haven't seen them around recently." Rachel looked concerned for a moment. *RECENTLY? THEY LEFT TREEFALL ALMOST THIRTY YEARS AGO!*

"Neal is back on Earth and just became a grandfather. He's a transport pilot, now, a simple run from Mars to Luna to Earth. Kept him at home so he can have a family."

"He's a grandfather? God, I'm starting to think that I myself might be getting a dog-eared. And Andy?"

"Still on Anteros, exploring the South." They were relatively secure in the northern continent and knew what to expect. The southern continent was still unexplored and full of surprises.

"Reckless. Andy was always too reckless," Dean carped. They looked at a large family of five, carrying their bags with two weeks' worth of clothes into the always busy Moyer Inn. "Everyone's coming in to hide under the blanket."

"Blanket?" Rachel asked. Dean tried to laugh, but couldn't --he went through a physical nodding motion, but he had simply outlived some of his most important functions, like laughing.

"It's an old term, Rachel. Your dad and I were up very late one night working on an idea he'd had, the high frequency acoustical emitter, to scare away the Leviathan Tree Howlers, which back then were killing a lot of settlers. I mentioned something like, 'we're just like kids ourselves, in a world where everything's a new experience.' Ben had said something about how little kids often hid under the blankets from the monsters in the darkness. I guess the name 'blanket' stuck and we used it for decades to describe the circular array of these emitters now over every settlement on Anteros. Each was designed exactly the way Ben had dreamed of many years ago."

"I'm surprised no one's thought of another idea."

"Nothing newer has been needed. Ben was always a bright one, especially when it came to tinkering with electrical things in his living room. Believe me, Rachel, his idea has saved a lot of lives, and he'd saved many more long before even moving here."

"Dad never talked about it."

"Didn't need to. I saw the pride and sense of accomplishment in his eyes. Ben didn't have that look for the first few months that he'd lived here, and needed to learn a lot about life in that first year. Every one of us close to him saw it was this process of awareness that truly mattered to him."

"You were all friends for sixty years,"

"Ben and Janice are my brother and sister, Rachel, and always will be. I do not have the words to describe just how much I care for them." Dean took on a mischievous look. Although his facial response was old and tired, Rachel still knew when

Dean was in a humorous mood. He leaned across the table.

"It's funny how Ben and Jan had always looked at me as some young, cocky kid, when all the while I was a few years older than both of them. I guess all of us were starting over back then. Ben and Janice were just trying to figure out who they were, but after being here for a while, they realized that what was most important was to love and live in the present."

THE END